CW00433340

The
Secret Library

Essential sensual reading

One Long Hot Summer

3 sensual novellas

One Long Hot Summer
by Elizabeth Coldwell

Just Another Lady
by Penelope Friday

Safe Haven
by Shanna Germain

One Long Hot Summer – Elizabeth Coldwell

Lily's looking after her friend, Amanda's, home on the Dorset coast, hoping it will ease her writer's block and help her get over her ex, Alex. What she doesn't expect is that Amanda's 21-year-old son Ryan will arrive at the house, planning to spend the summer surfing and partying – or that he'll have grown up quite so nicely. Ryan's as attracted to her as she is to him – but surely acting on her feelings for a man 14 years her junior is inappropriate? And when Alex makes a sudden reappearance in her life, wanting to get back together, should she follow her head or her heart? How can she resolve this case of summer madness?

Just Another Lady – Penelope Friday

Regency lady Elinor has fallen on hard times. The death of her father and the entail of their house put Elinor and her mother in difficulty; and her mother's illness has brought doctor's bills that they cannot pay. Lucius Crozier was Elinor's childhood friend and adversary; and there has always been a spark of attraction between the pair. Now renowned as a womaniser, he offers a marriage of convenience (for him!) in return for the payment of Elinor's mother's medical bills. Reluctantly, she agrees. But Lucius has made enemies of other gentlemen of the upper echelon by playing fast and loose with their mistresses, and one man is determined to take his revenge through Lucius's new wife ...

Safe Haven – Shanna Germain

Kallie Peters has finally made her dream come true – she's turned the family farm into Safe Haven, an animal sanctuary. But financial woes are pressing in on her, and she's worried that the only way to keep the farm is to allow her rich ex-boyfriend back into her life. When a sexy stranger shows up in her driveway with a wiggling puppy in his arms, she knows it's her chance for a hot rendezvous before she gives up her freedom.

The sex is hot, wild and passionate – the perfect interim before returning to the pressures of real life – but something else is happening between them. Can they find a way to save their dreams, their passions and their hearts, or will they have to say goodbye to all they've come to love?

Published by Xcite Books Ltd – 2012
ISBN 9781908262066

One Long Hot Summer
Copyright © Elizabeth Coldwell 2012

Just Another Lady
Copyright © Penelope Friday 2012

Safe Haven
Copyright © Shanna Germain 2012

The rights of Elizabeth Coldwell, Penelope Friday and Shanna
Germain to be identified as the authors of this work have been
asserted by them in accordance with the Copyright, Designs
and Patents Act 1988

The stories contained within this book are works of fiction.
Names and characters are the product of the authors'
imaginations and any resemblance to actual persons, living or
dead, is entirely coincidental.

All rights reserved. No part of this book may be reproduced,
stored in a retrieval system, or transmitted in any form or by
any means, electronic, electrostatic, magnetic tape, mechanical,
photocopying, recording or otherwise, without the written
permission of the publishers: Xcite Books, Suite 11769, 2nd
Floor, 145-157 St John Street, London EC1V 4PY

Cover design by Madamadari

Contents

www.xcitebooks.com

Scan the QR code to join our mailing list

More great titles in
The Secret Library

Traded Innocence
9781908262028

Silk Stockings
9781908262042

The Thousand and One Nights
9781908262080

The Game
9781908262103

Hungarian Rhapsody
9781908262127

One Long Hot Summer
by Elizabeth Coldwell

Chapter One – Blocked

HE KISSED ME FOR the first time in the shadow of the old pier, pushed up against one of the weathered wooden pilings. It seemed as though I'd been waiting forever to feel those soft, full lips of his pressing against my own, my body melting into the sweetness of his kiss. Above us, we could hear footsteps as people passed along the boardwalk, wrapped up against the early evening chill, oblivious to the way our passionate embrace was heating up the night.

His cock pushed at my belly, making its presence felt even through the layers of clothing separating us. I'd glimpsed his bulge earlier, straining against the crotch of his faded jeans, and I knew he was going to be big. I could hardly wait till I had that thick, delicious length in my hand, but something held me back from reaching to unzip him. That seemed far too brazen an act, even though we could no longer pretend we didn't want each other. Our desire had been on a slow burn since the day we met, and we both knew all it would take was another touch, another kiss to set it blazing out of control.

What he did next took my breath away. He –

'What?' I almost pounded the keyboard in frustration. 'What did he do?'

Staring at that last paragraph till the words threatened to blur into one didn't help. I'd been struggling with this chapter for weeks now, bereft of inspiration. This was the pivotal scene in the whole novel, the moment when my hero and heroine finally gave in to their overwhelming need and desire for one another. When I'd sketched out the initial storyline, I'd always had it in mind that they'd consummate their passion on the beach, beneath the old pier he'd first arrived in this sleepy seaside town to demolish. She'd fought against his grand scheme to redevelop the area, desperate to make him see he'd be destroying a vital part of the town's history and heritage, and in winning him round to her way of thinking she'd also won his heart. My editor loved the idea, and waited impatiently for me to deliver the completed manuscript. But for the first time in my writing career, I found myself blocked. The words wouldn't come, and when they did, they felt trite and predictable, a pale echo of everything I'd written before.

A change of scenery had been intended to cure the problem, taking me away from what I believed had caused it in the first place, but here I was, still no closer to finishing the novel. Giving up for the afternoon, I went down to Amanda's lavishly appointed kitchen to make myself yet another cup of coffee.

Waiting for the kettle to boil, I let my mind drift back to the conversation that brought me here in the first place.

The phone distracted me from reading and re-reading the draft of *Seafront Attraction*, wondering how to recapture the spark that invigorated the early chapters. If the words had been flowing, my fingers skittering over the keyboard and my concentration solely on the behaviour of my characters, I'd have let it ring. But answering it gave me the perfect excuse to step out of the box room I used as my study for a while, have a coffee, put on a load of washing, set the freezer defrosting – anything rather than return to my writing. In my current mood, I'd have been happy to chat to someone cold-calling in the hope of selling me a conservatory.

Rather than a salesman's dull spiel, Amanda's gushing tones greeted me. 'Lily. I do hope I haven't dragged you away from your writing?'

'No, not at all. I'd – er – come to a natural break in the story,' I replied, delighted to hear my best friend's voice. Amanda loved to gossip, and I prepared to settle in for a long conversation, pushing all thoughts of my overdue novel to the back of my mind. Her next words dashed those hopes.

'I haven't really got time to chat, darling. I found out this morning Roberto Almandi wants to show my work.' Without even giving me pause to ask who Almandi was, she continued, 'He only owns the hippest gallery on Manhattan's Lower East Side. You should see his client list. Woody Allen, Mickey Rourke. Madonna ...' No wonder she sounded so excited. As long as I'd known Amanda, she'd had ambitions of making it as an artist; instead, she'd found herself working in the press department of my publishers, Miller and Moore, which was how we'd first met. With the money she'd received in her divorce settlement from her husband, Duncan, she'd been able to devote herself to her painting at long last. Two years on, her work was being regularly exhibited; first at a gallery close to her Dorset home, then in London and now, it appeared, in downtown New York.

'Amanda, that's fantastic news.' Genuinely thrilled for her good fortune, I asked, 'When's the opening?'

'Eight days' time. Darling, I'm in such a hideous rush you wouldn't believe it. I've got to arrange transportation of the canvases, find a nice little *pied-à-terre* in which to stay while I'm over there ...'

'Oh, so you're going to be in the States for a while?' I'd assumed Amanda would attend the show's opening, give a couple of interviews, max out her credit cards in a Fifth Avenue shopping spree and return home. I should have known better.

'Lily, when will I get a better chance to spend some time in New York? Just think, opera at the Met, cocktails at the Algonquin, all those eligible men ...' Before she could get swept away in the full *Sex and the City* fantasy, she seemed to remember this was only supposed to be a quick phone call. 'Anyway, I'm looking at spending eight weeks there, maybe longer if I decide to take a trip to see New England in the fall. And I need someone to look after the house while I'm away.'

Amanda owned a beautiful beachside home a few miles outside Weymouth, on a stretch of what had become known as the Jurassic Coast. I'd been a frequent weekend visitor in the years we'd known each other, and I loved the place, with its secluded location and undisturbed view out over the English Channel.

'Won't Ryan be coming home for the summer?' Amanda's son, Ryan, was at university in the Midlands. She never failed to complain how he treated the house as his personal crash pad in the long vacation, arriving home with his washing and disrupting her peace by playing rock music in his bedroom at top volume.

'Not this year, darling. Ryan's informed me he has plans. He and a couple of friends are off backpacking round Thailand, apparently, while they wait for the results of their finals. Anything to put off getting a job just that little bit longer.'

I couldn't say anything, given that I'd become a world-class procrastinator over the last few weeks. 'So what will you do? Rent the house out?'

'Actually, Lily, I was wondering whether you'd come down and look after it for me. I'd much rather have you here than a load of strangers running around, drinking all my gin and prying in my knicker drawer. And, just as importantly, it saves me having to put Dexter in kennels.'

Amanda's eight-year-old German Shepherd crossbreed, Dexter, was another of the house's unique attractions. The dog had such a sweet, trusting temperament he was a pleasure to be around, and Amanda and I had taken him for many a long walk along the beach, throwing sticks for him to retrieve. I could see why she didn't like the idea of uprooting him from his home for such a long period of time.

I hadn't expected to be asked to house-sit, but the more I thought about it, the more the idea made sense. Everything in this flat still reminded me of Alex, even though we'd split up over six months ago now. The lease was up at the end of next month, and I'd been wondering whether or not to renew it, prone to nagging doubts that staying here, with all the memories of the times we'd shared together – good and bad – was contributing to my writer's block. How could my work move on if I couldn't? Amanda was offering me the perfect excuse to cut the ties that appeared to be holding me back, maybe even get out of London for good.

'I'd love to,' I told her.

'Wonderful, so it's sorted, then. Thanks, Lily. You've really got me out of a fix.'

Lying in bed that night, I couldn't help wondering whether I'd agreed to Amanda's surprising proposal too hastily. Cautious by nature, I liked to weigh up any potential situation, making a list of all the points for and against before I came to a decision. I'd done that when I hadn't been sure whether I was doing the right thing by giving up my job to write full time, and though Alex had never known, I'd done the same thing before moving in with him. How very different would my life be if, in both those cases, the column of cons had stretched further down the list than the pros?

Without meaning to, I found myself thinking back to the day Alex and I had moved into this flat, six years ago. One of the reasons I'd had on the list in favour of taking the plunge was that I'd been almost 30 at the time, that significant birthday looming like a milestone on the road ahead, impossible to ignore. Time to grow up, I'd told myself. Time to take some responsibility for my life. Another, far more important reason was that I couldn't bear to spend any more time apart from Alex than I had to.

His handsome, familiar face swam into my mind, crowned by unruly dark hair that fell into his soft hazel eyes, and with a slight dusting of stubble on his pointed chin. Impulsive and spontaneous, he'd been the one who'd suggested we take our relationship to the next level by finding a place together. When I'd agreed, he'd literally swept me off my feet in a huge hug, covering my face with kisses.

Almost without meaning to, I pushed back the bedcovers as the memory grew stronger, slipping a hand down to raise the hem of my nightdress up around my waist. Now I saw us on the day we'd moved in. We'd searched long and hard before finding what we considered the perfect home, a sunny garden flat close to Hampstead Heath. Newly refurbished, it boasted a brand-new, king-sized bed, and we hadn't been able to resist christening it before we'd even unpacked our possessions.

Alex carried me into the bedroom, placing me down on the bed. Only a couple of inches taller than me, he was deceptively strong, holding me in his arms as though I weighed nothing. 'Can't wait to make love to you,' he'd murmured. 'No distractions, no annoying flatmates. Just you and me, able to do whatever we want …'

He tugged my top off over my head, following up by flicking open the front catch of my bra, too excited to make any attempt at a long, slow seduction. Catching his mood, I fumbled for his belt, eager to take down his jeans and get my hands on the erection already pushing hard at the taut denim. Rolling over and over on the bed, each taking it in turn to have the upper hand, we quickly stripped each other down to nothing. Alex's cock, long and straight, almost begged to be clasped in my hand. Mouths locked together, Alex's fingers rolling my nipples into jutting peaks, we lost ourselves in our blind need to fuck and be fucked. Teasing Alex with steady pumps of my fist along his straining length, I brought him to the point where he begged to be inside me. Biting his lip, he almost whimpered as my thumb circled his cockhead, smearing the juice forming there over and around the hot, rubbery flesh.

'Oh God, Lily. I want you so much,' he groaned into my shoulder. 'Condom ... in my wallet ...'

Between the two of us, we fumbled his wallet out of his jeans pocket, the simple task of opening it and retrieving the condom made difficult by our both being so keyed up. My pussy was soaking, swollen and more than ready to take Alex's cock. If he'd pushed a finger into my entrance, I knew it would have slipped up there with almost shameful ease.

With Alex safely sheathed at last, we moved into our favourite position, me on top of him, straddling his firm thighs. He loved me to ride him like this, my pussy shifting up and down his length while he gripped my breasts or strummed my clit. We could gaze into each other's eyes, feeling the erotic charge of being so intimately connected, his flesh buried in mine. This chilly November afternoon, that charge was overwhelming. It made me move with an urgency I hadn't known I possessed, driving both of us to a swift, surging climax. Inner muscles clamping hard around Alex's shaft, I dragged his orgasm from him, hearing him cry out in passion, the words incoherent but the meaning clear. The play of emotions across his face as he pulled me into an embrace let me know just how good the sex had been. And, I was sure, it would only get better.

Reliving those bittersweet memories, my finger traced figures of eight over my clit, slicking my juices across the tight bud and bringing me to the point of orgasm in moments. Unable to stop myself, I rubbed harder, slipping the middle finger of my other hand up inside myself in the moment just before my climax hit.

When the last of the spasms died away, I realised there were tears in my eyes. Blinking them away, I vowed not to spend any more time thinking about what I'd shared with Alex. He'd put an end to all that the day he'd come home from work and told me he was moving out. Stunned, I'd begged for an explanation, but he couldn't produce one that satisfied me. There was no one else, he assured me repeatedly. In a way, I'd have found his decision easier to cope with if he'd admitted to having an affair. At least then I'd have a focus for all my negative emotions. Instead, he said that, as far as he was concerned, what there'd been between us had simply run its course, and by leaving now, rather than letting things drag on, he'd spare me the pain of reaching the same realisation myself. That evening, he gathered together all his possessions, called a cab and went to stay at a friend's house. He hadn't been back to the flat since.

Alex had made the break; now it was my turn. By moving into Amanda's home for the summer, I could finally put our relationship in the past. In new surroundings, with a positive new outlook, I'd be able to finish *Seafront Attraction* and deliver it to my editor.

At least, that had been the plan. Standing in Amanda's kitchen, wondering if there were any biscuits left in the tin or whether I'd have to top up my supplies at the village shop tomorrow, I couldn't help wondering where things had gone wrong. I still couldn't finish the damn novel. Maybe I never would, though the consequences of that didn't bear thinking about. Something had to change for the better; I simply didn't know how to make it happen.

Chapter Two – Ryan

WAKING TO THE SOUND of rain pattering hard against the bedroom window, heralding another disappointing day in what had been a pretty miserable summer so far, I revised my plans to go shopping, deciding to do a spot of baking instead. In the days when I'd occasionally hit a brick wall in terms of whatever I was writing at the time – as all writers do – I'd found spending time in the kitchen, kneading dough or mixing cake batter, a sure-fire way to start my creative juices flowing again.

Today, it was just another way of avoiding turning on my PC. Checking my emails when I'd got off the phone to Amanda, I'd found a chatty message from Robyn, my editor, asking how I'd settled into my new home, and how *Seafront Attraction* was coming along. I'd sent a bland little reply, letting her know she'd have something very soon – and how many times had I told that same lie over the last couple of months? – but I couldn't help feeling guilty. I counted Robyn as a friend; we'd had a great working relationship throughout the years she'd been editing my novels, and I could only imagine the pressure she was under to get my latest book to print.

Measuring butter and sugar into a mixing bowl, beating it with a wooden spoon till the muscles in my upper arm ached and the mixture was light and fluffy, I tried not to think about Robyn, or anything to do with my unfinished novel. I'd always enjoyed making cakes; maybe I should forget about writing, and reinvent myself as one of those women who opens an exclusive bakery selling fancy cupcakes at eye-watering prices? After all, Amanda had got out of publishing to follow her dream of being a painter, and look at how successful she'd been. But writing *was* my dream, the one thing I loved more than anything else.

Aware my thoughts were running in circles, like a hamster endlessly making circuits of a wheel, I added nuts and chocolate chips to my cookie dough and spooned it on to a greased baking sheet. While the cookies baked, I had time to nip upstairs and check my messages again. I really owed it to Robyn to send her a more honest assessment of how things were going. Perhaps she could offer me advice on what to do next; Lord knew I didn't have a clue any more.

Twenty minutes later, I came back downstairs having, I hoped, made my peace with Robyn. The appetising smell of warm sugar and vanilla hit my nostrils. It should have lifted my mood, but a noise coming from the kitchen put me on edge. Dexter's barking, loud and sharp. When I'd left him, he'd been dozing in his basket, soothed by the warmth of the oven. Now, he sounded agitated. Something had to be wrong.

Pushing open the kitchen door, an unexpected sight greeted me. The fridge stood open, and a man was peering into it, while Dexter paced beside him, tail wagging as he continued to bark. I couldn't see the stranger's face, but I could pretty much see every last inch of his tanned, lithe body, as all he wore was a pair of white trunk underwear. I'd read news reports of burglars who'd made themselves a snack while in the process of robbing a house, but I couldn't imagine any thief going about his business in such a state of undress. So who the hell was he, and why was he treating the place like he owned it?

Wondering whether I should alert him to my presence, I couldn't help letting my gaze drift to where those trunks clung to the firm contours of his backside. Friend or foe, this man had the most spectacular arse I'd seen in a long time.

The bleeping of the kitchen timer, letting me know the cookies were ready to come out of the oven, saved me having to speak. The intruder turned at the sound, startled, and in that moment I recognised him. His hair was longer than I remembered, sun-bleached blond strands falling into his smiling blue eyes, and the stubble on his chin indicated he hadn't shaved for a day or so, but it was unmistakably Ryan. When I'd last seen him, a good three years ago, he'd been a gawky sixth-former, still not quite at home in his body following a growth spurt that had pushed him to six feet in height. Now, though, he'd filled out very nicely indeed, his frame tapering from broad shoulders to lean hips, with a stomach that, while toned, didn't bear the hard ridges of muscle to suggest he spent most of his free time working out. Just the kind of body you could trail your tongue along, all the way down to the package emphasised so enticingly by that tight-fitting underwear …

I pulled myself up sharply at the thought. This was Ryan, my best friend's 21-year-old son, and a lad a whole 14 years younger than me, not the hunky hero of one of my romance novels. Though, for a moment, I didn't think it was only in my imagination that his eyes made the same slow, appraising circuit of my body as mine had made of his.

'Hey, Lily!' His grin was crooked, appealing on a purely sexual level, and I couldn't help being glad Amanda hadn't insisted on giving me the courtesy title of "aunty", as so many women do with their close female friends. 'What are you doing here?'

'I could ask you exactly the same thing. Aren't you supposed to be in Thailand?'

'That was the plan.' Ryan leant against the now closed fridge door, watching as I retrieved the sheet of cookies from the oven. 'Except Charlie didn't manage to sort out his passport in time and it all kind of fell apart. So we decided to come down to the coast for the summer.'

'We?' I looked round, wondering whether any more half-naked young men were about to step out of the shadows and make their introductions.

'Yeah. Charlie and Giles are staying in a B&B down the road in Weymouth. They were hoping to crash here, but I told them Mum had someone looking after the house. I didn't realise it was you.'

'So what would you have done if it had been someone else?'

'Oh, I dunno.' Ryan waited only seconds after I'd placed the cookies on a wire rack to cool before coming over to the table to snaffle one. Breaking off a piece and popping it in his mouth, he chewed thoughtfully. 'Probably gone off to join them. But I'm sure you don't have any problem with me staying here, do you? These are delicious, by the way.'

He didn't sound as though he was trying to charm me by complimenting my cooking. And I had no intention of suggesting he leave, now he was here. It would be nice to have another body around the house, seeing as my plan to capitalise on the solitude the beachside cottage offered to finish my novel had already come unstuck. Though if he intended to meet up with his friends, I probably wouldn't see all that much of him. Certainly not as much as I could see right now …

Stop it, I told myself. OK, so it's been a while since you've been in the company of someone you found so attractive, and your sex life could best be filed under "non-existent", but there are limits.

'Do you fancy a coffee?' I asked. 'I was just about to make one.'

'Great,' he replied. 'I'll just go and put some clothes on. I was about to have a shower, but …'

But what? *That can wait? That would be more fun if you joined me?*

'Back in a mo,' Ryan said chirpily, and left, treating me to one last view of his delectable arse, cheeks flexing beneath the tight white cotton.

In his absence, I busied myself grinding coffee beans – another trick I'd adopted to waste time, rather than buying the ready-ground variety – and boiling the kettle. As I watched raindrops chase each other down the window pane, my overheated imagination picked up the idea of stepping into the shower with Ryan, not caring how inappropriate such thoughts might be given the difference in our ages. I pictured him peeling down those tight trunks that had done so little to conceal the dimensions of his cock. In my fantasy, it reared up, hard and proud, its plump head already shining with juice. I fought the urge to reach out and stroke my fingers up and down its solid length.

Beneath the towel knotted just below my armpits, I was naked, and I undid the knot, opening the towel wide to let Ryan feast his eyes on my small, high breasts, curvy hips and the soft red curls on my mound, a couple of shades darker than those which fell halfway down my back in wild profusion.

The shower in Amanda's bathroom had a cloudburst head, and being pulled beneath its spray by Ryan was like finding myself caught in a tropical storm with him. I loved the effect, feeling the water beating down hard on our bodies as he pulled me into a close embrace. Our lips met, the scratch of Ryan's stubble against my cheeks adding another level of stimulation to my increasing arousal.

Slowly, I dropped to my knees, my tongue trailing down his smooth, wet chest, over the flat plane of his belly and down to where his cock waited for my oral caress. Holding my damp curls out of the way with one hand, I used the other to grip the base of his dick, keeping him steady so I could take his crown between my lips. He filled my mouth to the brim, the salt tang of his precome waking my taste buds, making me hunger for more. Swirling my tongue over his straining flesh in sloppy circles, licking at the sweetly sensitive spot where the head meets the shaft, I brought a sharp gasp of pleasure from him. Looking up, letting him all but fall from my lips, I saw his eyes screwed tight and his head thrown back, fat drops of water raining down on his exposed throat. In that moment, he looked so masculine, yet so submissive, his whole body taut and trembling, waiting for me to plunge my head back down on his cock. What could I do but oblige, using my hand to wank him with slow, steady tugs that couldn't fail to have him coming within moments, shooting his load to the back of my throat as I swallowed it in quick, greedy gulps.

The image I'd created was so vivid I could almost feel the water raining down on my bare back, taste the last, salty drops of Ryan's come. When had I lost the ability to put those feelings, the overwhelming emotions of making love to such a gorgeous young man, on paper? I shook my head to clear it of the lingering remnants of my fantasy, aware of a tell-tale wetness in my panties.

By the time Ryan returned to the kitchen, dressed in a pale pink T-shirt bearing the name of its designer on the front and a pair of baggy, knee-length khaki shorts, the coffee had brewed and I'd made a mental note to get fresh batteries for my vibrator the next time I went shopping. I poured a mug and handed it to him. He dumped a couple of spoonfuls of sugar in it, stirring vigorously, before taking a sip.

'So how long were you planning on staying?' I asked. 'Not that I'm trying to get rid of you, or anything.'

He grabbed one of the kitchen chairs and turned it round, sitting on it so his elbows rested on the top of the chair back and his thighs straddled the seat. 'Not sure yet. Could be a month, could be longer.' Reaching for another biscuit, he broke it in two, throwing one half to Dexter, who crunched it up greedily. 'The plan's for us to do some surfing, but that all depends on the weather and the tides. I mean, we can always go over to Bournemouth – there's a great spot down by the pier - but it gets so packed with tourists. And then there's Kimmeridge Bay, just the other side of Weymouth, but the conditions there are so inconsistent, you never know what you're going to get. So I reckon we should hire a boat and hit some of the places only us locals know about ...' He broke off, concerned that my eyes appeared to be glazing over. 'Hey, Lily, I'm not boring you, am I?'

I shook my head. 'Of course not. It's just been a while since I had a conversation with anyone other than Mrs Bentley in the village store, that's all. I'm relishing the novelty of not discussing the weather, or how much butter's increased in price since my last visit.'

'Well, why don't you tell me what you're doing here, out in the back end of nowhere? How did Mum persuade you house-sitting for her would be a good idea?'

'To tell you the truth, I didn't need any persuading. It gave me the chance to get out of London for a while. I needed a break from where I'd been.' Wondering whether I should tell Ryan the whole story or not, I decided there was nothing to lose by pouring my troubles into his sympathetic ear. 'You see, the relationship I'd been in for a long time had broken up ...'

'Were you still with that Alex guy?' Ryan interrupted. About to ask how he knew about Alex, I remembered that we'd come down to stay with Amanda one glorious April weekend. If I remembered rightly, Ryan had been revising for his A levels at that point, his maths text books strewn over this very kitchen table.

'Yes, that's right. Well, we went our separate ways a few months ago.'

'That's a shame. He was a really nice guy, from what I remember. Drove a Triumph Spitfire, didn't he?'

'He still does. What a memory you've got.' The classic, cherry red sports car was Alex's pride and joy. Every time I walked along the street and failed to see it parked outside our flat, I received a painful reminder that he was no longer in my life. 'Well, when your mum suggested I come down here, I thought it would be an ideal opportunity to get away from my old life and really concentrate on my writing for a while, with no distractions.'

'And how's the writing going?'

It was an innocent enough enquiry, but I still felt an anxious clutching in my gut at the thought of the unfinished manuscript on my PC. 'It's OK, all things considering.'

'Meaning you don't want me getting under your feet while you're trying to work.'

'Oh, I don't see you being any trouble. Not if you're out with your friends all the time.'

Ryan's next comment saved me having to outline the full horror of my insurmountable writer's block.

'So tell me more about what it is you write. Mum's got a whole stack of your books in her bedroom, but when I asked if I could read one of them, she always used to say she'd let me when I was old enough.' Again that slow, sexy grin, causing something to come unglued deep inside me. 'Am I old enough now?'

'I should think so, but they're really aimed at women.'

'Isn't all the best erotic fiction?' Ryan chuckled, and I felt a flush rise to my cheeks. A tinny electronic tune filled the air, sparing me from further inquisition. Ryan dug in his shorts pocket as the tune repeated itself, bringing out his smartphone. 'Hey, Charlie, how's it going? Yeah, yeah … It's an old friend of my mum's, Lily Metcalfe. Oh, she's cool, she's a writer … Yeah, I'm sure you'll get to meet her. OK, see you there.'

'Are you off out?' I asked, not wanting to speculate on what questions might have been asked about me on the other end of the line.

'Yeah, I'm going to meet the guys in Weymouth.' Ryan stood, pulled his car keys out of his pocket, tossed them in the air and caught them. 'I should be back early evening.'

'Oh, that's fine. I've no intention of keeping an eye on your comings and goings, not even if your mother asks me to.' A thought struck me. 'Does she actually know you're here?'

He shook his head. 'Not yet. I'll get round to telling her eventually.'

'Won't she be checking for photos of your Thai adventures on Facebook?'

'I'm not sure Mum even knows what Facebook is. And even if she did, I've blocked her from accessing it.' Pure wickedness infused his grin. 'You've got to keep some things secret from your folks, after all. See you later, Lily.'

With an affectionate ruffle of Dexter's fur, he was gone, heading for the elderly green Mini parked by the side of the house. I didn't stop to see him pull away, turning out on to the road that led to Weymouth. I was still wondering whether Ryan's appearance had derailed my plans for the summer – and if that might, in the long run, turn out to be a good thing.

Chapter Three – Reading

THE EMAIL POPPED INTO my inbox a little before six o'clock. *"On way home. What's for supper? Ryan x"*, followed by an automated line to say the message had been sent from his smartphone. I was torn between admiring his cheek at expecting me to feed him and a sudden giddy rush at the prospect of seeing him again. This wasn't like me, acting like an overgrown schoolgirl in the presence of a man I found attractive, I told myself sternly. But hadn't that been the same reaction Alex had always provoked from me in the early days of our relationship, when just the sound of his voice on the phone could get me wet?

Just as well I'd gone with my instincts and put a chicken in the oven earlier, I thought as I logged out of my mailbox and went downstairs. If Ryan got back late, there'd be leftovers if he wanted to make himself a sandwich. As it was, I'd be serving it with potatoes baked in their jackets and a crisp green salad – and maybe a glass or two from the nice bottle of Chilean Sauvignon Blanc chilling in the fridge.

By early afternoon, the rain had passed over and I'd been able to take Dexter for his walk. Even on the sunniest days, the beach here was never busy, being just a little too far for most day trippers from Weymouth or Bridport to venture. Today, with the clouds still low and threatening and the sand damp and cloying beneath my boots, I had the whole bay pretty much to myself, able to let Dexter off his leash to run out into the sea, paws splashing in the surf as he barked at the seagulls who bobbed on the waves.

Returning to the cottage, I still had no enthusiasm to work on my novel, so instead I spent an hour or so updating my blog, adding the recipe for the chocolate and nut cookies I'd baked that morning as I knew I always got extra hits when I discussed food. Sex and chocolate - the two things guaranteed to attract readers, I'd mused, before reaching for my ideas notebook and scribbling down a note about finding a storyline that linked the two. And if ideas were starting to pop into my head, I thought with an optimism that had been lacking over the last few weeks, it couldn't be long before I was struck with the compulsion to write once more.

Around 40 minutes after I'd received Ryan's message, I heard a car pull to a halt on the gravel driveway at the side of the cottage. Moments later, he strode through the front door, Dexter rising from his basket and trotting out into the hall to greet him.

'Hey, Lily, something smells good,' he said, entering the kitchen.

'Thought I'd cook a chicken for tonight, and your timing's great, because it's just about ready.'

'You know when I asked what was for supper, I was joking, right? Honestly, I don't expect you to feed me while I'm here.'

I returned his grin with one of my own. 'I'm feeding myself. If you want to join me, you're more than welcome.'

Though I'd been relishing the chance to be on my own when I took on the job of house-sitting for Amanda, it somehow felt right to have Ryan sitting at the table, piling his plate high with salad and spreading a generous amount of butter on a slice of home-made granary bread.

'This is fantastic,' he said, clinking his wine glass against mine. 'Thanks, Lily. I was expecting to have to open a can of beans when I got in.'

'You're not much of a cook, then?'

'I can find my way round a grill pan, but most of the time, I live on takeaways. Mum always despairs that I never inherited her love of cooking, but maybe you could give me a few lessons, if you have the time?'

Oh, there are plenty of things I'd love to teach you, and cooking's pretty low down the list, I thought, but I answered him with a simple nod. 'Yeah, that shouldn't be a problem. So how was Weymouth?'

'Great. Turns out Charlie and Giles are staying with a real old battle-axe. She's got strict mealtimes and curfews, so there's no chance of them sneaking girls up to their rooms, which is what they were hoping for.'

'I thought they were just here for the surfing?'

'Well, yes, but there are some girls who really go for a man on a surf board. Maybe it's the wetsuit, maybe it's the danger and the adrenalin rush, who knows?' Ryan made to top up my glass; I let him pour a couple of inches of wine into it before stopping him, not wanting to drink too much tonight. My tongue had a tendency to run away with me when I'd been drinking; it was how I'd first found the courage to tell Alex exactly how attractive I found him, and all the things I'd like to do to him if I ever got him alone.

Forget about Alex, a little voice in the back of my head warned me. You'll never be able to move on if you can't stop dragging him into every situation, and after all, isn't that why you're here? To leave the past behind, once and for all?

As if to make up for his outstanding lack of culinary ability, Ryan offered to do the washing up. I left him up to his elbows in hot, soapy water, scrubbing the roasting tin clean of chicken grease, and went to curl up on the living room sofa. Amanda wasn't a great one for gadgets, as Ryan had implied with his comment about Facebook, but she had treated herself to satellite TV, and I flicked through channel after channel in search of something to watch. By the time Ryan joined me, I'd settled on an old Woody Allen film, in which a couple become convinced their neighbour has murdered his wife. I'd seen it before, but I loved the sharp, bantering dialogue – like all writers, I was a sucker for lines I wished I'd written – and the central performances from Allen and his leading lady that really did make you believe they were a long-married, indulgently bickering couple. I wondered if Ryan might prefer something with a few more special effects and car chases, but he settled down in the armchair opposite me and quickly became engrossed in the increasingly ludicrous events on screen, laughing along in all the right places.

When the end credits rolled, I turned to Ryan, to ask whether he fancied a coffee. He shook his head. 'I'm off to bed, if it's all the same to you. I got a text from the boys while I was in the kitchen. Apparently the weather forecast for tomorrow is perfect for surfing, so I'll be away from here at the crack of dawn.'

'OK. Sleep well.'

Ryan pulled the living room door shut behind him as he left. I wandered through to the kitchen, stifling a yawn as I did. Grabbing an early night suddenly sounded like a really good idea, so I reached for the jar of hot chocolate lurking at the back of the cupboard and made myself a cup to take up to my room.

As I passed Ryan's room on the way to my own, I thought I could hear a low, groaning sound. Pausing on the landing, wondering if I'd been mistaken, I heard it again, a little louder this time. It sounded as though he was in serious pain. If that was the case, did he need me to call a doctor?

The door to his room was slightly ajar. Peering round it, the most unexpectedly erotic sight met my eyes. Ryan lay on his bed naked, the covers pushed down past his ankles. One hand gripped his cock, shuttling rapidly up and down its length, which glistened with some kind of lubricant. In the other, he clutched a dog-eared paperback book. He must have been close to coming, for his breath was laboured and from time to time he let out a groan, just like the ones I'd heard before. Groans that, far from being a sign of illness,

21

showed just how aroused he was.

My pussy quivered with desire, and I fought the urge to slip a hand up my denim skirt and massage it through my panties. I shouldn't be spying on Ryan at such an intimate moment, I knew that, but I just couldn't help myself. I'd never seen anything so horny in my life.

It wasn't as though the sight of a man wanking was alien to me. I'd watched Alex make himself come on a number of occasions, but then he'd been putting on a deliberate show for me, just as I – and now I didn't try to submerge the memories that pushed, hot and enticing, to the front of my brain – would use my Rabbit vibrator on myself for his viewing enjoyment. What I watched now was all the more horny because it was private, Ryan pleasuring himself for no one's gratification but his own.

His hand moved faster, the pumping motion more desperate now, and I couldn't help myself. My fingers snaked under the hem of my skirt, making contact with the damp crotch of my underwear and pushing it to one side, so I could stroke a finger over the slick, hot flesh beneath. Ryan's back arched against the mattress and he let out a despairing shout, as though he couldn't hold his climax back a moment longer. Clearly unable to concentrate on anything but the orgasmic sensations pulsing through him, he tossed the paperback to one side.

Despite my lust-fuelled haze, I wondered what he'd been reading that might turn him on quite so powerfully. Catching sight of the book jacket where it had fallen, I fought to stifle a whimper of my own. The Gothic lettering in which the title was rendered and image of a black-haired woman, face contorted with lust, dress falling to bare one shoulder, was all too familiar.

Pagan Instincts; the first novel I'd had published and still one of my favourites. It told the story of an archaeological dig on the site of an old Viking burial ground, and the relationship that developed between Scarlett, one of the students on the dig, and her course tutor, Professor Archer, a man with a taste for bondage and submission games. Ryan had obviously borrowed it from Amanda's bookshelves, curious to learn the secrets of my fiction following our earlier conversation. I wondered which scene he'd used to get himself hard and horny; maybe the one where Archer had bound Scarlett's wrists to the bedposts for the first time, and repeatedly brought her to the verge of orgasm, until she was begging him to let her come. Or perhaps the one where she'd allowed him to slowly strip her naked in front of the other male members of the dig, as proof of her willingness to submit to him.

There wasn't time to dwell on the many thrilling possibilities, as at that moment Ryan's pleasure crested and he cried out as he came. I couldn't be sure, but the word he uttered at the peak of his ecstasy sounded an awful lot like "Lily".

That seemed to break the spell. Certain if I stayed where I was any longer I'd do something to draw Ryan's attention to me, and not liking to think what the consequences might be if he caught me peeking, I tiptoed away down the landing to my own room.

Making sure the door was securely shut behind me, I undressed, not bothering to slip into my nightdress. The mug of hot chocolate was left to go cold on the nightstand. All I could think of was the sight of Ryan, fist a blur on his thick, luscious cock as he brought himself off, spurred on by the erotic power of my writing. Had he been imagining me in the same position as Scarlett, hands tied behind my back and my mouth full of virile man-flesh? Did he long for me to bare myself for his hungry gaze, just as Scarlett had bared herself for the professor and his colleagues? Or was I simply reading too much into the situation, and if he hadn't had my book to hand, he'd simply have conjured up a memory from his own private wank bank to satisfy his urges?

I didn't care. All I knew was my pussy was suffused with

prickly heat, and I needed to come. Plunging two fingers up into my juicy channel, relishing the liquid heat I felt there, and the way my inner muscles gripped them tightly, I stroked my clit with the pad of my thumb. Shivers of lust coursed through my belly with the delicious friction. I didn't need to weave an elaborate fantasy to take me over the edge; mind flashing back to the sight of Ryan, naked and abandoned as he writhed against the bedsheet, I sobbed with the sweetness of the orgasm that rippled through me.

I'd never tell him what I'd seen, of course, and as I gave in to the pleasant sleepiness that followed my orgasm, I made a mental vow to keep my distance. Desire had struck me hard – but I told myself firmly that desire was misdirected. Cute as Ryan was, he was too young for me, strictly off-limits, and refusing to acknowledge that could only lead to heartache.

Chapter Four – Sweltering

JUST AS HE'D PREDICTED, when I woke the following morning, Ryan had already left to meet his friends. They'd been right about the weather; pulling open the bedroom curtains, it was to see that, at last, summer had arrived in a glorious blaze of sunshine. Already the day held the promise of heat to come, and I decided that, rather than stay cooped up indoors, I'd take my notebook and a cool glass of lemonade outside. Inspiration was bound to strike in the shade beneath the apple trees at the bottom of Amanda's garden.

It shouldn't have come as any surprise that instead of picking up where I'd come to a shuddering halt in the manuscript of *Seafront Attraction*, I found myself scribbling down notes about a character who was thoroughly at home on a surfboard. Resisting the temptation to make him lean and blond, with a crooked grin and the ability to charm the birds down from the trees, I made him a professional surf champion, self-sufficient and focused on nothing but winning. At the top of his game, he'd suffer a potentially career-threatening injury taking part in a competition. Of course, there'd be a sympathetic nurse on hand to look after him – no, I could almost hear Robyn's voice telling me just how clichéd a combination that was. So maybe a physiotherapist, whose job was to help him learn to walk again? Now, that had promise; his spiky personality would rub against hers, but somewhere among their battling and her refusal to give up on him, love would blossom ...

Dexter's tongue licked the back of my hand. I glanced at

my watch to see I'd been working for the best part of two hours, and I had a more than serviceable outline to send to Robyn. It didn't help me meet my overdue deadline, but at least it proved I hadn't lost my creative abilities. After the frustrations of the last couple of months, it counted as serious progress.

'You hungry, boy?' I asked, patting Dexter's shaggy back. 'OK, let's go feed you.'

Spooning a tin of gravied chunks into Dexter's bowl, I heard the front door slam, followed by a babble of loud male voices. The kitchen door was flung open and Ryan bounded into the room, followed by two other lads of around his age.

'Oh hi, Lily. Hope you don't mind Charlie and Giles dropping by. Hey, Dexter ...' Ryan bent to make a fuss of the dog. His hair was damp, and he wore a short-sleeved neoprene top and matching shorts that left his tanned, muscled calves bare. His friends were dressed in similar fashion, radiating the same air of youthful energy, and I couldn't help giving them a cursory once-over. Charlie was taller than Ryan and long-limbed, with dark hair that even the waves hadn't been able to dislodge from its thickly gelled style and strangely delicate features for such a big man. Giles had tousled, sandy curls and an angular face, with a nose that had been broken at some point, more than likely in a tumble from his surfboard. Everything about the way they spoke and held themselves suggested an upbringing aided by quiet wealth. I wouldn't be surprised to learn that either or both of them had a trust fund providing the money to pay for this last, indulgent summer before the world of work sucked them in.

'You're back earlier than I expected,' I commented.

'Well, we'd found a great spot a couple of miles down the bay,' Ryan replied, 'but the wind's dropped and the waves just aren't forming the way we'd like. So we decided to call it day. I came to drop my board off and then we're heading into Weymouth.'

'Can I get you a drink?' I asked. 'There's some lemonade in the fridge, home made.'

'Thanks, Lily, that would be great.' Giles was already pulling open the fridge door. 'Ryan says you're a bit of a star in the kitchen.'

'I don't know about that,' I replied, watching with amusement as the lads poured themselves glasses of lemonade and downed them with big, greedy gulps. I should have been annoyed at their sudden intrusion on my peaceful working environment, but I wasn't. When I'd first agreed to look after the cottage, I'd never thought I'd welcome this sudden explosion of noisy masculinity, but anything that brought Ryan into my orbit for even a few minutes was fine by me.

Drinks finished, glasses rinsed in haphazard fashion under the tap, the boys decided it was time to go.

'See you again, Lily!' Charlie waved over his shoulder at me as they left the kitchen. Dropping his voice, so I wasn't sure whether he intended me to hear his next remark or not, he muttered to Ryan, 'Mate, she is a total MILF!'

'Yeah, you've fallen on your feet having her in the house,' Giles added. 'You know what they say about older women.'

No, I wanted to ask, what do they say? But he declined to elaborate. Instead, Ryan said, 'Oh, come on, she's my mum's best friend. I've known her for, like, for ever.'

'And that makes a difference how, exactly?' Charlie asked. 'Come on, Ryan, if you had the chance, would you?'

The front door slamming shut cut off Ryan's reply. I realised now how his friends saw me, based on their first impressions – and it was all positive. On one level, it was nice to be considered a potential bed partner; my confidence had taken a huge knock when Alex walked out on me, and I'd almost stopped thinking of myself as desirable. But some kind of lusty cougar, on the lookout for fresh young prey ... That wasn't how I viewed myself, and I suspected Ryan felt

27

the same.

But if that was the case, why was I suddenly so disappointed? Was I really hoping that my fantasies weren't so wide of the mark after all, and Ryan wanted me just as much as, deep down, I wanted him?

This was silly, I told myself with sudden firmness. Ryan might be my dream toy boy, but he certainly wasn't the right person to become involved with, not after all the hurt Alex had put me through. I needed something simple, uncomplicated – not a summer fling with a much younger man, however enticing the thought of hot, passionate nights in Ryan's arms might be. I'd come to the coast to work, not to party, and now I'd at least made a start at tearing down the mental wall that barred the way to completing my novel, to throw any of that progress away would be foolish.

Losing myself in my writing didn't prove quite as easy as I'd hoped, not with Charlie and Giles becoming increasingly frequent visitors to the cottage. While Ryan was off surfing, or taking long, rambling walks along the coastal path with Dexter at his heels, I was able to concentrate on my new work in progress, which I'd titled *Off The Lip*, one of the surfing terms I'd picked up from the boys' scatter-gun conversations on the subject. Creating characters was always my favourite part of the process, and in Jayden Shaw I had the perfect alpha male hero. Successful, arrogant and, of course, almost improbably handsome with his sun-bleached hair, chiselled profile and lean surfer's build, he was simply asking to run into a woman who could stand up to him. That woman was Meredith James, intelligent and feisty, powerfully attracted to Jayden despite professing to hate him. Their growing desire created sparks of erotic tension whenever they were together. It wasn't a scenario that would challenge the boundaries of literary fiction, but it offered the escape from reality and happy-ever-after ending readers looked for whenever they picked up one of my novels.

Every morning, I'd take up my spot under the apple trees, seeking shade. The warm weather had settled in with a vengeance, and each day the mercury in the thermometer rose just a little further, temperatures creeping higher into the eighties. Already the TV forecasters were predicting this July would be one of the hottest on record, with no sign of a break in the weather.

The lads had settled into a routine, Ryan setting off at seven every morning to pick up his friends so they could chase the best surfing conditions along the coast. More often than not, early afternoon would see them descending on the cottage to grab a bite to eat. Their arrival usually signalled the end of my working day; by then, it was too hot to do anything but take a cool bath and settle down for a siesta. The oppressive heat was making it hard to sleep at nights.

Or perhaps that had more to do with thoughts of Ryan, sleeping just along the landing. He still had no idea I'd seen him playing with himself the evening he arrived, or that he'd been using one of my books to turn him on, but I'd kept an eye on the bookshelves in Amanda's room, and noticed that *Pagan Instincts* had been returned to its place in her collection, only for Ryan to borrow *Shadow Play* and *Staged Seduction* in turn. It seemed he liked what he'd read in that first novel enough to go back for more.

Lying in bed, tossing and turning beneath the thin sheet that was all I could bear to cover myself with on these sticky nights, I couldn't help imagining what it would be like to push open the door of Ryan's room, catching him in the act of stroking his cock. He'd be embarrassed at first, but I'd assure him he had nothing to be ashamed of, pressing a finger to his soft, full lips. *We all do it*, I'd tell him, leaning forward so he could gaze down the front of my nightdress, where he couldn't fail to notice the way my nipples poked forward, tight and anxious for his touch. *But sometimes it's more fun to let someone else do it for you.* And my hand would replace his on his thick shaft, pumping it with slow, even strokes.

Or maybe I'd take him into my mouth, swallowing him more deeply than anyone had before, till he was buried in the soft cavern of my throat. I'd know tricks girls of his own age hadn't even heard of, or would be too afraid to try, like getting my finger nice and wet, running it over the tight, untried entrance to his arse before gradually pushing it inside. The combination of my sucking lips and probing finger would have him exploding in ecstasy within moments, telling me no one else had ever done that to him, and it seemed so wrong but it felt so right.

All just fantasy, of course. Something to get me through these long, sleepless nights, nothing more. It didn't make it any less enjoyable; I just had to remind myself there was no chance of it becoming reality.

'So it is OK if Giles and Charlie stay for supper tonight?' Ryan asked, coming into the kitchen where I stood chopping vegetables for a stir-fry, my stand-by meal whenever I was catering for more guests than I'd expected.

'Of course,' I told him. 'They're welcome here any time, you know that. You should be able to invite who you want. After all, it is your house.'

'I know, but I don't want to put you to any trouble.' He looked so adorable, with his hang-dog expression, part of me longed to drop a kiss on the end of his nose and tell him to stop worrying.

'It's no trouble, honestly. If I hadn't wanted to cook, I'd have made you order in a takeaway. Now, if you want to be useful, there's a packet of egg noodles in the left-hand cupboard …'

Fifteen minutes later, the four of us sat round the kitchen table, tucking in to beef, vegetables and noodles, jazzed up with a slug of sweet chilli sauce.

'This is delicious, Lily,' Giles said, his manners impeccable as ever. 'Thanks for cooking for us.'

'Thanks for providing the alcohol,' I replied. The lads had turned up with a dozen bottles of pilsner-style lager, produced by a craft brewery on the outskirts of Bournemouth. Those we hadn't yet got round to opening waited in the fridge, making it obvious they were planning to spend at least part of the evening here.

'So,' Charlie gestured at me with his fork, 'Ryan says you're a writer, and you're here working on a book at the moment. But he didn't say what kind of thing you write. Anything I should have heard of?'

'Oh, they're romance novels. Not the most highbrow reading for an English graduate like you, I'm afraid.'

'But they are very horny,' Ryan chipped in. A blush spread across his face as he realised he was in danger of giving the secrets of his nocturnal reading away, and he quickly amended, 'That's what Mum says, anyway.'

'So how come you boys aren't off out on the town somewhere?' I asked. 'After all, it's Friday night. Isn't that when all the action happens round here?'

Ryan took a swig from his lager bottle before replying. 'Everywhere's just so packed at the moment, and it's too hot to go clubbing. I mean, there's working up a sweat and working up a sweat ...'

'Which is where Lily's books come in, eh, mate?' Giles grinned at his own remark, and I knew he and Charlie weren't going to let up until they found out quite how closely Ryan had studied my work.

Our plates were empty, and I rose to clear them from the table and load them into the dishwasher. 'Oh, we'll do that,' Charlie assured me, taking the plates from me. 'It's the least we can do.'

'Well, if you're in the mood for dessert, there's a tub of ice cream in the freezer. White chocolate and raspberry.'

'Maybe later,' Ryan said. 'Why don't we all get more beer and go through to the living room, eh?' His look made it obvious I was included, and I took another bottle of lager from him with a grateful smile.

We made ourselves comfortable in the living room. Somehow, I found myself on the sofa, Giles to my right and Charlie to my left. Ryan went over to an expensive looking sound system and hunted through the rack of CDs stored beneath it, tutting at his mother's choice in music. At last, he found something that appeared to be to his liking. He slotted it into the machine, and an Ibiza chill-out tune filled the room, soft and hypnotic.

Coming back to join us, he stretched out on the floor at our feet. Charlie handed him an opened bottle of beer, and he raised it in a salute. 'This is the life,' Ryan announced, before placing the bottle to his lips.

'So you wouldn't rather be in Thailand?' I asked, thinking about the boys' original plans for the summer.

'It would have been fun,' Giles said reflectively, 'but they've got nothing to speak of in the way of surfing over there.'

'Yeah, you've always got to weigh up the pros and cons,' Ryan added, his words reminding me of the thoughts I'd had before coming here. When I'd made the decision to house-sit for Amanda, I hadn't expected I'd ever find myself relaxing in her living room with three fit, intelligent and funny men barely in their twenties – and fighting a wholly unsuitable attraction to the hottest of the three – but here I was, sipping from my beer and feeling thoroughly at home.

'Why don't we play a little game?' Charlie asked.

'What did you have in mind?' My tone was wary, expecting him to respond with "strip poker", or something equally predictable.

He must have known there were lines I wasn't prepared to cross, for he replied, 'I was thinking of a round of true confessions. We take it in turns to reveal the most outrageous thing we've ever done. Are you all up for that?' We nodded. 'OK, who's going first?'

'I will,' Giles replied. 'It happened last summer, when we

went down for that weekend in Rock.' The Cornish town he referred to was the biggest party destination for young people with money who wanted to surf, have casual hook-ups and dance till dawn on the beach. It struck me as Giles' natural stomping ground. 'It was the first time I've ever done a hang 11.'

'A what?' I asked, baffled.

'You know what a hang ten is, Lily?' When I shook my head, Giles enlightened me. 'You stand right on the edge of the surfboard with all your toes hanging off the end. It's a tricky manoeuvre, but not impossible. Well, I got talking to this Aussie guy, Jarrod, who told me if you do the same thing stark naked, it's a hang 11.' He paused for a moment, allowing the implication to sink in. 'So I thought I'd give it a try.'

An image flashed into my mind: Giles, stripping out of his wetsuit and climbing on to the board, paddling out till he hit a suitable wave, then getting into the required position to ride it home. His cock would be as sturdy as the rest of him, and I was certain he'd been quite a sight, if anyone had been around to watch his antics.

'Fun?' Ryan asked.

'Mate, it was amazing. You've got to try it. There's nothing like rolling round in the surf naked, especially on a hot night.'

'Well, that's nothing,' Charlie said. 'The most outrageous thing I've done is have sex in the stacks of the university library.'

'Seriously?' Ryan looked at Charlie with wide eyes, as though he suspected his friend of lying.

'Yeah. It was the final term of our second year. You lot all had exams to study for, but I had to write a dissertation. Ten thousand words on the unreliable narrator in 20th century literature. Anyway, it meant spending a lot of time in the library, and I'd left most of the work I had to do until right at the last moment. I don't know if you remember, but at the time, there was a really cute library assistant working there, Kendra. Scottish, with long, black hair and a sexy giggle. Had the most spectacular tits and used to wear these tight T-shirts that showed them off a treat.' He smiled at the memory.

'And that's who you fucked?' Giles asked, a trace of envy in his voice.

'Yeah. I was working late one Friday night, and I mean really late. I had about three days to go before I was due to turn the dissertation in, and I still had a whole section on *The Turn of the Screw* to write.' He swigged from his bottle. 'But I suppose you know all about what it's like to be up against a deadline, Lily.'

If only you knew, I thought, but I simply nodded.

'Well, I must have been the last student in the place, because suddenly Kendra's at my elbow, telling me it's gone ten o'clock and I should be thinking about leaving. She was looking particularly hot that night, in this low-cut pink top that left most of her breasts exposed. I tell you, I could have crawled into that cleavage and stayed there for the rest of my life. But I just powered down my laptop and started stuffing my course notes into my bag. That's when she put her hand on my arm and told me that, actually, she'd quite like me to stay.

'Now, I know a come-on when I hear one, and Kendra and I had been giving each other these flirtatious looks for weeks now, so I was pretty sure where all this was heading. If I hadn't got the hint by that point, she left me in no doubt about what she wanted when she slithered down to her knees and kissed my cock through the fly of my jeans.'

By now, you could have heard a pin drop in the room. Giles and Ryan were hanging on Charlie's every word, and even I was anxious to know how the story would end.

'Part of me still thought this was a dream, that I'd nodded off over my text books and any minute now the old dragon of a head librarian would come over, wake me up and tell me to go home to my digs. But when Kendra pulled my zip down and guided the head of my cock into her mouth, well, I knew this just had to be real. Nothing had ever felt so good as those soft lips of hers surrounding my knob, and the way her tongue flicked over the tip – oh, man!

'I'd have happily stood there and let her suck me off till I came, but she had other ideas. After a couple of minutes of licking and slurping my length, she let me drop from her lips, then draped herself over the desk I'd been working at, looked at me with this real saucy expression on her face and said, "Fuck me, Charlie." As blatant as that.'

'And you didn't worry that someone might come and catch you at it?' Giles asked.

Charlie shook his head. 'My dick was doing all my thinking for me by then. Wouldn't yours have been? But even though they had security patrols on campus overnight, I doubt they ever ventured down as far as the library stacks.' He paused, took a swallow of beer. 'I haven't even told you the best bit yet. When I flipped Kendra's skirt up and went to pull her knickers down, I got the surprise of my life. She wasn't wearing any. Now, I don't know whether she'd gone into the ladies' and removed them before coming to find me, or whether she'd been bare beneath that little skirt all day. The thought of her climbing ladders to put books on the highest shelves, giving anyone who cared to look a glimpse of her naked pussy – well, if I'd had any indication she'd been dressed like that when I arrived at the library, I wouldn't have got a stroke of work done all day.

'Luckily, I had condoms in my wallet, otherwise it would have meant a dash upstairs in the hope the vending machine in the toilets was working. Kendra wriggled her arse at me while I rolled one on my cock, letting me know just how keen she was to have me inside her. So I got behind her, parted her pussy lips with my fingers and guided myself home. It was like sinking my dick into wet silk; I could feel the heat of her through the condom, and she was making all these little moans and whimpers as I started to fuck her. She told me she wanted me to go as hard and deep as I could, and what a lady wants, a lady gets, right? After a couple of strokes to get used to the feel of her, I started really slamming in hard, pushing her against the table with every thrust. Kendra was bucking her arse back at me, and I knew I wasn't going to hold out very long, buried in her tight cunt and hearing her urge me on with some seriously dirty talk. "Do it, Charlie," she kept saying. "Give me a fucking I'll never forget.""

I listened, rapt, to Charlie's story. The way he told it, I could see the two of them in my mind, Kendra's long hair flying around her face in wild abandon, Charlie holding her hard by the hips and thrusting deep into her welcoming pussy, buttock muscles flexing hard with every stroke. It was the kind of fast, spontaneous sex I hadn't had in longer than I cared to remember, and my pussy had grown damp in response to his tale. I looked over at Ryan, and for a moment our eyes met. His expression was unreadable, but I was sure if I glanced at his crotch, I'd see a definite bulge there.

'Another few strokes was all it took,' Charlie admitted, bringing his tale to its conclusion. 'Kendra had her fingers in her crotch, rubbing her clit, and I felt her pussy clutch hard at my cock as she came. The orgasm I had, feeling her milk every last drop of spunk from me, almost blew my head off. I'm surprised they didn't hear the noise I was making clear across campus.

'When it was over, I gave her a kiss, we got dressed and went our separate ways. The next time I went in the library, the following Monday afternoon, I couldn't see Kendra anywhere. When I asked after her, I was told Friday had been her last day on the job. I suppose you could say I'd been her leaving present.'

Charlie sat back, gauging our reaction to his adventure. Giles was shaking his head in disbelief, not quite sure whether he believed what had happened or not. Ryan shifted in his seat; like me, he couldn't fail to be aware of the growing tension in the room, and the feeling that, with each story, the stakes were being raised.

'So who's next?' Charlie asked. 'Go on, Ryan, why don't you tell us the most outrageous thing you've ever done?'

Ryan shook his head. 'There isn't much to tell. I don't know that I've ever done anything to compare with your exploits.'

'Oh, come on, mate,' Charlie urged him. 'There has to be something – or someone – that stands out in your mind.'

Thinking about it for a long moment, Ryan finally said, 'Well …'

Just as he was about to launch into his story, the phone rang on the other side of the room. The sound made me jump, and I realised I'd been holding my breath in anticipation of hearing all about some secret part of Ryan's past.

Rising to my feet, I said, 'I'd better go and see who that is.'

'Just check the caller ID,' Charlie suggested. 'If you don't recognise the number, let the answerphone pick it up and Ryan can get on with telling us his story.'

'It's not my house,' I reminded him gently. 'I don't recognise any of the numbers.'

The number flashing on the call screen had an 00 1 area code. That meant America; more specifically New York. Amanda had been in touch from that exact number at least twice a week since she'd flown out for the gallery opening.

I picked up the handset, knowing she would expect me to be alone and waiting for her call. 'Hi, darling!' She sounded positively chirpy. It was hardly surprising. Given the time difference, it was late afternoon over there. Cocktail o'clock, Amanda would have called it.

'Amanda, how are you?' The mention of her name was like a cold downpour in the steamy atmosphere of the living room. Giles immediately gathered together the empty beer bottles, preparing to dispose of them, while Charlie started hunting under the coffee table for the flip-flops he'd kicked off when he'd sat down.

'Fine, fine. You wouldn't believe how well things are going over here.' From the tone of her voice, this was going to be no quick social call.

Ryan caught my eye and mouthed the word, 'Coffee?' I nodded, and he disappeared in the direction of the kitchen.

'So, tell me all about it,' I said, taking the phone handset over to the sofa and curling up on the cushions with my legs tucked underneath me.

'Well, the reaction to the exhibition has been incredible. Roberto says he's never seen anything like it …' I'd noticed as the weeks had gone by, Amanda had dropped Roberto Almandi's name into the conversation with increasing frequency. He'd been prominent on the photos of the party held to mark the opening of Amanda's exhibition, and with his aquiline features and shock of ash-blond hair, I knew he was just her type. Her relationship with him hadn't yet moved from strictly professional to something more intimate, otherwise I'd have heard all the juicy details by now. 'He's even talking about extending the exhibition by another fortnight, just to maximise the sales potential. Tells me it won't be long before anyone who's anyone is clamouring to own an Amanda Carter original. And would you believe I've sold one of my reclining nudes to none other than Janie Lee Richmond?'

'That's great,' I replied, reeling slightly under the volley of information, 'but who is she, exactly?'

'Oh, Lily, don't tell me you haven't heard of her. She presents the Channel 8 morning show, with the guy who was on *Celebrity Survival Island* – you know the one. Anyway, I was a guest on the show last week, and Janie Lee loved my work so much, she went straight down to the gallery that afternoon and wrote out a cheque for *Study In Blue*. Said it'd look perfect hanging on the wall of her penthouse on Central

Park West. But more importantly, how are you? Getting all the peace and quiet you need?'

'Well, I've been doing some writing, if that's what you're asking.'

'Darling, that's marvellous. I can't wait to read that novel of yours when it's out in print.'

You're not the only one, I thought, given the speed with which Ryan's working his way through my backlist.

'Everything else here is fine,' I told her. 'The weather's good, Dexter's getting plenty of exercise …'

'Lovely. But tell me, you haven't heard from Ryan at all, have you?'

That was the exact moment Ryan chose to return to the living room, coffee mugs in hand. He placed one down on the table and I gave him a little wink in gratitude. I needed to phrase my words carefully. Amanda still didn't know her errant son had come home for the summer; as far as she was concerned, he was partying the night away on a beach on Koh Samui.

'If I do,' I told her, 'I'll be certain to let him know that he should drop you an email.' I looked directly at Ryan for the last part of the sentence, making sure he got the hint.

'Thank you so much. Sometimes I think he forgets he's got a mother at all … Oh, I'll have to go. I've got a call waiting on the line and I think it might be Roberto. Speak to you later, Lily. 'Bye.'

With that, she put the phone down.

'How is she?' Ryan asked.

'Very well,' I replied, 'but maybe you should find that out for yourself. You don't have to tell her you're not in Thailand; just let her know you're still alive.'

Aware I was in danger of sounding more like his mother than Amanda did, I took a sip of my coffee, registering a strong aftertaste of whiskey. 'Wow, there's a kick to that!' I exclaimed.

'I thought you might need it if you were on the phone to

Mum.' Ryan grinned. 'You know what she's like when she settles down for a chat. I never ring her unless I know I've got at least two days' worth of supplies to hand …'

We were still laughing when Charlie popped his head round the door. 'We're going to scoot off,' he said. It seemed Amanda's unexpected phone call had killed the party mood. 'We've put the dishwasher on, so you don't have to worry about that, Lily. Thanks again for dinner. See you tomorrow, Ryan.'

With that, he and Giles left the house. Charlie drove a dirt-streaked old Land Rover with a couple of surfboards lashed to the top. Ryan and I stood on the doorstep and watched him back it a little recklessly down the driveway and on to the road.

I couldn't help wondering what might have happened if Amanda hadn't rung when she had. Ryan would have shared his story with us, and then it would have been my turn. What would I have told them? Maybe I'd have confessed to the night I fucked Alex at a stuffy dinner party thrown by his boss, feigning a headache and giving Alex five minutes to join me in the guest room, where he'd gone down on me while the other diners ate their beef Wellington, oblivious to our antics.

Somewhere along the way, I'd lost that wild sense of mischief. Spending time around Ryan and his friends, still so spontaneous and carefree, reminded me how much I needed to put the fun back in my life. Maybe I should join the boys for a morning's surfing? I'd never as much as held a surfboard, but they could teach me the basics between them. It might even prove useful research for my new novel.

Shaking my head, deciding that might be just a step too far, I turned to make my way back inside the house. Ryan reached out and caught hold of my hand, sending a giddy thrill through me.

'Lily, I – I just wanted to say thank you,' he said, his blue eyes fixed on mine.

'For what?'

'For not ratting me out to Mum. You didn't have to do that.'

'And what would it have achieved if I had?'

'Well, I know you came here to be on your own. I can't help feeling we're getting under your feet.'

'Not at all – and if you were, do you think I'd have agreed to cook dinner for everyone?'

'No, and I really appreciate that. So do Charlie and Giles. And we'll make it up to you somehow, I promise.'

'Oh, there's no need for that,' I assured him. Just having Ryan in the house had such a positive impact on my writing; I could no longer imagine being here all alone. But of course I couldn't tell him that. The less I told him about how I felt, the better for both of us.

Chapter Five – Party

'I'M THROWING A PARTY on Friday night,' Ryan said as he passed me in the hall, lugging his surfboard out to the car. Our paths had barely crossed in the past week. He'd been leaving the house early and coming back late, and I'd been locked away in my makeshift study, the free-standing fan Ryan had brought down from the attic working overtime to cool the air as I polished the first three chapters of *Off The Lip*, ready to send them to Robyn. Of course, there was still the small matter of finishing *Seafront Attraction*, but one thing at a time.

'Ah. Now I know why your mother's blocked from following your Facebook updates. You don't want her to know you're inviting a load of complete strangers over here to trash the cottage in her absence.'

'Hey, not fair!' Ryan retorted. 'They're not strangers. They're all our surfing buddies – oh, plus a couple of girls Charlie was chatting up in the pub the other night – and we're going to have the party on the beach. Get a barbecue going, set up a sound system …'

'Annoy all the neighbours …'

'We've thought of that. We're going to invite them too. That way, they can either bring a bottle and join in, or they've had fair warning and they can make plans to be somewhere else.'

'And this is my fair warning, is it?' I asked, thinking I'd go into Weymouth and have dinner on Friday evening, maybe catch the new Hugh Jackman film at the local cinema.

'No, it's a request for your presence. We want you at the party.'

'Oh, I don't know about that. I don't think I'd exactly fit in with a bunch of surfer boys?'

'Are you kidding? It won't be the same without you. Say you'll come, Lily?'

Ryan stared at me with big, puppy dog eyes and something deep inside me melted. 'OK. Yes, I'll come. Why not? Maybe it is time I let my hair down for once.'

'Oh, just one last thing,' Ryan said in the moment before he slammed the front door behind him. 'The dress code for the party is strictly swimwear.'

People started arriving for the party around nine on Friday. Not surprisingly, after receiving their invitations our nearest neighbours had both decided to be elsewhere for the evening. Ryan had spent the last hour or so setting up a fire pit on the beach, close to the cottage, and the scent of grilling chicken, heavy with lemon and garlic, wafted on the air. The sound system he'd mentioned when he'd been planning the party turned out to be an old-fashioned boom box, playing dance tunes whose heavy bass lines floated out on the still night air.

Cars parked on the road outside the cottage, disgorging little knots of partygoers clutching six-packs and bottles of cheap cider. Once they'd navigated the zig-zagging cliff path down to the beach, Ryan took the offerings from his guests. He plunged the cans and bottles into the old tin bath we usually used to wash Dexter, which had been filled with ice to keep the drink cool.

I sat on a blanket, close to the low cliff, nursing a plastic cup of white wine as I watched Ryan laugh and joke with his friends. I'd been apprehensive when he'd told me the dress code was swimwear. It was an obvious choice – on a hot night like this, who wouldn't be tempted to spend at least part of their time in the water? Ryan wore nothing but a pair of baggy blue shorts, and the sight of his nicely muscled body, tanned a couple of shades darker than when he'd first arrived by the summer sun, made me yearn to run my fingers over the firm planes of his shoulders and chest. But I wasn't too keen on wearing something revealing myself, not when all the other female guests would be nearly half my age. I didn't have a bad figure – being tugged along by Dexter as he pulled at his lead on his walks gave me all the exercise to balance out my sedentary working habits – but I doubted I could compete with their youthful bodies and sun-kissed skin. With my red-headed, Celtic genes, I struggled to achieve any kind of tan. Instead, I simply cultivated the pale and interesting look.

Mostly, the girls arrived with slouchy T-shirts thrown over their bikinis – if a couple of triangles of fabric held together with string could be classed as a bikini, that was. I'd wrapped a floral sarong round my hips, feeling more comfortable with that extra coverage. Ryan hadn't mentioned a girlfriend, or even anyone he was interested in among the girls who hung round the surfing crowd, but that didn't mean he hadn't invited someone here tonight with the intention of hooking up with her.

'Hey, Lily!' I looked up to see Giles standing before me, clutching a can of beer. He swayed slightly, as though he'd already had a drink more than was good for him. 'Come and dance with me.'

I shook my head. 'I don't think so. This isn't really my kind of music.'

'Oh, come on.' His tone was beseeching. 'I hate to see you sitting there on your own, when you should be having a bloody good time like everyone else.'

I thought about trying to convince him I was having a good time, then wondered what I really had to lose. Draining the last of my wine, I clambered to my feet and followed Giles over to the patch of sand where half a dozen people were dancing. The music changed to an uplifting, trancey tune that made me want to twirl slowly on the spot, revelling in the feeling of being alive and surrounded by happy people on such a glorious night. I hadn't had more than a cup of wine, but at that moment I guessed I was just high on life, using a phrase that would have made me cringe in other circumstances.

I thought I caught sight of Ryan watching me, the look on his face one of amusement and something like admiration, then a couple came to dance alongside Giles and me, blocking him from my view. The girl by our side had wild corkscrew curls and skin the colour of caffè latte, and I noticed Giles giving her a lustful glance, his eyes lingering on her barely-clad backside even after the man with her pulled her into a tight embrace, dancing in a suggestive fashion that had more to do with his evident need for her than the beat of the music.

I couldn't help grinning. 'So … Got your eye on anyone in particular tonight?'

He shook his head. 'Just thought I'd leave it to fate and see what happens, you know? But Charlie's after the blonde in the black one-piece.' Giles gestured in the direction of the girl he meant with the hand that still held his beer can. 'She's the barmaid at The Dolphin; that's the pub we usually go drinking in. I keep telling him she's got a boyfriend and he's got no chance, but you know what Charlie's like. Nothing if not determined.'

'And what about Ryan? Is he chasing anyone?' Despite myself, I had to know.

'Ah – now that's where it gets really interesting.' Giles leant close. 'I know I shouldn't be telling you this, and if he asks, don't say you heard it from me, but there's only one woman in Ryan's heart.' Giles broke off as the music segued into something more frantic, driven by a pounding drum-and-bass rhythm. 'Oh, man, I love this tune!'

'Giles.' I did my best to drag his concentration back to the matter in hand. 'You were about to tell me who it is that

Ryan likes.'

'Well, she's not a million miles away from here, I'll say that much.'

'Giles? Come on, don't tease me like this,' I begged.

'OK, here's your second clue.' He pointed at me and winked.

'What?'

'Yeah, that's right, Lily. He's got the hots for you, big time. But I think the whole "you being his mum's best friend" thing makes it a bit tricky – at least for him. I keep telling him he should do something about it. I would if I was him, because you're fucking gorgeous.' He went to take another swig from his can, seeming baffled to find he'd already emptied it. 'I need another one of these. Can I get you anything?'

'I'll come with you, sort you out a plate of food,' I told him, guiding him through the mass of dancing bodies in the direction of Ryan's fire pit. We'd have some serious cleaning up to do tomorrow, I thought, even though we'd already left out a couple of black bin bags where people could toss their empty cans and discarded chicken bones. But I'd worry about that later. For the time being, I was too busy wondering how to deal with the bombshell Giles had just landed on me.

The best way to do that was to stay out of Ryan's path for a while, just till I'd digested all the implications. Even as I decided that, I heard a familiar voice at my ear. 'Hey, Lily. Enjoying yourself?'

'Oh, hi, Ryan. Yeah, I'm just trying to get some solid food into Giles. Otherwise he'll be sleeping his hangover off on the beach.'

'Well, it wouldn't be a proper party otherwise.' He reached for a paper plate, piling it high with chicken legs, Cumberland sausages and a hunk of French bread. 'There you go, mate,' he said, handing it to Giles.

'So how come you've ended up manning the barbecue?' I

asked. 'I'd have done that for you.'

'Sorry, barbecuing is strictly a man's job.' He grinned. 'Never come between a bloke and his slightly charred shish kebabs or there'll be hell to pay. Have you never read *Men Are From Mars, Women Have Impossibly High Standards*, or whatever it's called?'

Giles, having grabbed another beer, caught my eye and gave me another significant wink, inclining his head in Ryan's direction before plonking himself down on the sand and tucking into his food.

'Mind you,' Ryan continued, 'I wouldn't mind getting away from the grill for a few minutes.' He called over to a short, dark-haired lad in his early 20s who was rummaging through the impromptu cooler in search of a drink. 'Hey, Chrissy, you wouldn't mind manning the barbie while I take a bathroom break, would you?'

'Sure thing, mate,' Chrissy replied in a strong Australian accent.

Expecting Ryan to make his way up to the cottage, I was surprised when, instead, he started walking down the beach towards the water's edge. When he beckoned me to follow him, I did, trotting to catch up with him.

'I thought you needed the bathroom?' I asked.

'No, but I knew if I gave that excuse, Chrissy wouldn't fail to take the reins. I just wanted to get away from everyone. We've not really had the chance to talk all evening, and I wanted to be sure you're enjoying yourself. I mean, this isn't really your usual crowd, is it?'

'Are you saying I'm an old fuddy-duddy?'

He shook his head. 'No, but I can't help thinking you've already done a lot of partying when you were my age, and you're probably bored of it now.'

Looking out to sea, where the full moon's reflection was captured and held by the waves, I replied, 'I was never really the party-going type back then. But I'm having a good time tonight. Giles can be very entertaining when he wants to be.'

'Yeah, can't he just?' Ryan grinned. 'I saw the two of you having a bit of a heart-to-heart earlier. Nothing serious, I hope?'

'I don't think Giles is capable of being serious. No, we were just talking about random stuff. Like who Charlie fancies – and you.'

'Me, really? What did you have to say? Anything interesting?'

I knew I was in danger of making a fool of myself, of spoiling the easy friendship we'd built in the last few weeks, but I didn't care. Maybe I'd been infected with a case of summer madness. Whatever the cause, something about the moon on the water and the muted sounds of the party, music and voices far enough away to let me know there was no danger of our being overheard, made me bold. 'OK, Giles was telling me there's a woman you like, but you don't want to let her know because the situation's a bit complicated. But the truth is she already knows how you feel, because she feels the same way.' My eyes locked with his, and I took a breath, not sure I wanted to know what his reaction was going to be.

Ryan didn't say anything at first, and I was sure I'd blown it. I wouldn't be at all shocked if he told me he was going to pack up his things and go and join Charlie and Giles in the B&B. Then he took an awkward pace forward. In that moment, as we stood looking at each other, I became aware just how much bigger and broader than me he was. 'Oh, Lily,' he murmured, and brought his mouth down to meet mine.

His lips were soft, and his mouth tasted of the red wine he'd been drinking. I raised myself on tiptoes, wrapping my arms around his neck. Ryan pulled me to him, hands clasping my sarong-clad backside, and I could feel his cock starting to stir into life, pushing at my belly through his shorts. All the doubts I'd had about whether we should be doing this, wondering if it was inappropriate to act on my desire for a younger man, melted away under the onslaught of his kiss.

By the time we finally broke the kiss, I felt breathless and light-headed. Ryan's face dissolved in a grin, as though he couldn't believe quite what he'd done.

'That was nice,' I told him. 'So nice I think we should do it again.'

Ryan obliged, his kiss just as strong and passionate as before, then his mouth moved on, lips nibbling softly at my earlobe before seeking out the sensitive spot on the side of my neck. He held my hair away from my skin, licking and lapping a wet trail down to my collar bone. By that time, I was squirming against him, my pussy liquefying, my whole body on edge and desperate for more intimate caresses.

Part of me wanted him to just lay me down on the sand and fuck me, but that wouldn't have been the most sensible idea. Everyone was still clustered on the makeshift dance floor, but that didn't mean someone might not have the bright idea of coming down to the sea to cool off, and the last thing I wanted was to be caught with Ryan's cock buried in my pussy.

'Maybe we should take this inside?' I suggested. 'That is – if you want to?'

'I've never wanted anything more,' Ryan assured me. Taking me by the hand, he led me back up the beach. No one paid us any attention as we passed: Charlie had made his move on the blonde barmaid, and was muttering something in her ear, making her giggle in response. Giles and Chrissy were standing at the barbecue, no doubt discussing the finer points of how you grilled a burger without reducing it to charcoal. Everyone else was far too busy drinking or dancing to notice Ryan guiding me up the cliff path, towards the empty cottage.

We slipped in through the kitchen door. Dexter, snoozing in his basket near the oven, roused himself briefly at the sound of Ryan's voice, before giving a little whine and settling back down to sleep.

I'd never felt as giddily excited as I did climbing the stairs, hand in hand with Ryan. It seemed everything that had happened since I'd walked into the kitchen and found him standing there half-naked, hunting through the fridge, had been leading to this moment. We'd tried to fight our feelings and failed, and now we'd surrendered to the inevitable.

'Your room or mine?' I asked, as we stood on the landing.

'Mine, I think,' Ryan said. 'Unless you've got a stash of condoms in yours that I don't know about.'

Now there was no doubt how this was going to end. After all, he wouldn't have mentioned condoms if he wasn't going to use them.

Pushing open the door, he took me into his room. I'd had a glimpse of it before, of course – and he still didn't know about the night I'd spied on him, I realised with a pang of guilt – but I'd never been inside until now. The expected litter of dirty clothes, used tissues, and bits of surfing equipment was nowhere to be seen, and I wondered briefly whether he'd straightened the place up in the hopes of bringing someone back here tonight. Or maybe he was just the naturally tidy type.

When he kissed me again, I stopped thinking about any neat-freak habits and concentrated solely on the feel of his tongue battling with my own. My fingers twined in the short ends of his hair, and I sighed at the delicious feeling of his hard cock pressing against me. He tugged at the halter neck of my bikini top, searching for the snap fastening; when he popped it open, the two halves of the top fell forward, baring my breasts to him.

'Oh, Lily, you have the most gorgeous breasts.' Ryan's tone was awed, as though he was looking at a priceless work of art. 'I love all the cute little freckles on them.'

He traced over those freckles as he spoke, before using the tip of his finger to tease my nipple. The bud, already tight with need, stiffened even further at his touch, and I moaned out loud.

'Oh, so sensitive ...' Ryan switched his attention to the other nipple, drawing the same reaction from me with very little effort.

'Please,' I murmured, though I wasn't sure quite what I was asking for.

He glanced down at my bikini top, hanging uselessly around my waist. 'Take it off, Lily,' he said, the words more of a command than a request. 'Take it all off.'

Did my gorgeous toy boy have a dominant streak? I wondered, as my hands flew to the back fastening of my top, pulling it apart, before undoing the knot that held my sarong in place. The silky material slithered to the ground, leaving me standing in a pair of bikini bottoms considerably more substantial than the other girls at the party were wearing.

Ryan didn't say a word, just waited for me to remove those too. He couldn't have failed to notice the dampness in the crotch as I peeled them down, or the briny scent of excited woman that permeated the air.

'God,' he murmured, the would-be master almost reduced to speechlessness by the sight of my naked body. Recovering himself, he said, 'I've fantasised about this moment so many times, but I never thought it would be so good.'

So it wasn't just my writing that fuelled his masturbation sessions, then. 'And what else have you fantasised about?' I asked. 'Because maybe that'll be better in real life as well.'

'I – I think about you sucking my cock,' Ryan admitted.

He didn't need to say another word. I slid to my knees before him, my face a perfect mask of submission and longing as I caught hold of the waistband of his shorts. When I'd tugged them down to his ankles, he stepped out of them. I tossed the garment to one side, not caring where it fell. All that mattered was my first glimpse of his cock, as long and hard as its insistent presence against my stomach had suggested, with a strong upward curve. The hair around it hadn't been lightened by the sun the way that on his head had, and when I moved closer, taking his shaft in my hand, I could smell the enticing, earthy maleness of his crotch.

My fist moved in a lazy, pumping action up and down the length of him, easing back his foreskin from the plump head that already shone with a little precome. 'Are you ready for this?' I asked him seductively.

'Yes,' he replied. 'Oh, Lily, please don't tease me ...'

'Haven't you learned yet that the anticipation makes it all the sweeter?' With that, I circled his crown with my lips, the touch so light as to frustrate him further. He jerked his hips, wanting to push himself further into my mouth, but my hand at the root of his cock held him steady. I didn't want this to be over too quickly, even though I had the feeling he'd come in my mouth whatever I did, the potency of his deepest desires made flesh too much to resist.

Somehow, though, he held back, even when I took him fully between my lips, my tongue flicking over and around his cockhead. I didn't know how it compared to his fantasies, but it was every bit as exciting as I'd always hoped it would be, my mouth full of his hot, musky flesh, my free hand gripping at his thick thigh to steady myself as I worked my lips and down his shaft.

The moment he feared he was about to come, he pulled back. 'I need to fuck you so much,' he said. 'Need to know how it feels to be buried deep in your pussy.'

'Then do it,' I told him, sitting on the bed and patting the space beside me, inviting me to join him.

Those condoms he'd mentioned were in the top drawer of his bedside cabinet. He fetched one, and I rolled it slowly into place, the gesture simply another excuse to keep touching and stroking his gorgeous cock.

Once I was satisfied with my efforts, I reclined back

against the pillows, spreading my legs and making it obvious I wanted him between them. Ryan crawled up the bed, looking at me as though all his Christmases had come at once. Now there was a thought; Christmas in July, with the temperature, at this late hour, still up in the seventies. And the heat we'd generated between us was nudging the mercury even higher; beads of sweat glistened on Ryan's chest, and I ached to lick them up.

Instead, I pressed my lips to his as he leant over me, catching fistfuls of my curls and slowly manoeuvring himself into place as we continued to kiss. When his latex-sheathed cock bumped against the entrance to my pussy, I reached out and guided him in. Not so big as to be uncomfortable, he still stretched muscles that hadn't received much of a workout since Alex left me, and I let out a tormented groan.

'I'm not hurting you, am I?' Ryan asked, eyes wide with concern.

'No. It – it's just been a while, that's all. Please, don't stop, whatever you do.'

Happy to obey, Ryan shoved harder until he was snugly buried in my wet channel. He gazed down at me, lust shining in his blue eyes, and in that moment it didn't matter that he was 14 years younger than me, that I'd been at university while he was in primary school, that most of my favourite bands had split up before he'd even been born. The connection between us was so strong, so vital, it made those differences irrelevant. We were meant to find ourselves here, joined on the most primal level, my legs wrapped around the small of his back as he started to fuck me with short, shallow thrusts. Why try and fight that?

'Oh, Ryan, that feels good,' I told him, urging him on to move a little faster, push a little deeper, hitting the neglected spot high up on my pussy walls that responded best to firm pressure.

'It feels even better to be inside you,' he replied.

My nails raked at the skin over his shoulder blades, passion rising at a pitch that threatened to run out of control. Already, Ryan's movements were losing some of their fluency as he got more excited, closer to coming. I needed more stimulation if I was to follow him over the edge, and I murmured in his ear, 'Touch me. Make me come.'

Maybe he'd never been with someone who'd issued such a direct request, and at first he didn't quite know how to respond. Then he dropped a finger to the place where his body joined with mine, finding my clit where it peeped out from the slick folds of skin surrounding it, and gave it a gentle rub.

It seemed as though my world dissolved at his touch, and I could only call his name helplessly, lost in the sensations of my orgasm. Even when I closed my eyes, I could still see Ryan's gorgeous face, teeth biting at his lower lip as he tried to hold his own orgasm back just a few seconds longer. But my squeezing, clutching pussy muscles were stronger than his willpower and, with a despairing roar, he came in a series of little jerks.

His kisses were soft as he eased himself out of me, slipping from the bed to go and dispose of the condom. I watched him cross the carpeted floor, eyes drinking in the sight of his bare back and arse. Part of me still couldn't quite believe we'd just fucked; it felt like a glorious dream brought on by the wine and the summer heat. But the faint soreness in my muscles and the languor in my limbs told me it was all deliciously real.

Maybe tomorrow we'd have to talk about what we'd done, and what might happen if – or, more likely, when – his friends found out. And what would I say to Amanda? But those were problems for another time. Now, as Ryan joined me once more and I snuggled into the crook of his shoulder, all I could do was try and stay awake for long enough to watch his own eyes close and his breathing change to soft snores. I barely managed it, then all the excesses of the day overtook me and I couldn't fend off sleep any longer.

In my dreams, I was dancing on the sand again, body moving to the loud, thumping rhythm of the drums. Except the thumping was coming from somewhere close by, dragging me awake. Someone was banging on the front door. In response, Dexter barked, the sound urgent and excited.

The sun slanted through a crack in the curtains, already strong enough to suggest it was mid-morning. I hadn't heard any of the guests departing, so I had no idea what time the party had finally come to an end, or quite how long Ryan and I had slept. Untangling myself from Ryan's sleepy embrace, I went over to the bedroom window and pulled the curtains open, looking down to see who was on the doorstep. The red Triumph Spitfire parked at the kerb couldn't fail to tell me the identity of my mystery caller.

Alex.

Chapter Six – Alex

'WHAT'S HAPPENING?' RYAN ASKED, sitting up in bed as I grabbed his striped towelling bathrobe from where it hung on the back of the door.

'Alex is downstairs,' I told him, pulling on the robe and fastening the belt securely at my waist. It was far too long for me, the sleeves reaching all the way down to my fingertips, but I didn't have time to look for anything more suitable.

It took a moment for what I'd told Ryan to register. 'What, you mean your ex-boyfriend Alex? What's he doing here?'

'I have absolutely no idea, but I'm about to find out.'

With that, I hurried out of the room, taking the stairs as fast as I could without tripping over the hem of the bathrobe. When I opened the front door, Alex's fist was raised, as though he was about to hammer on the wood one last time. He looked at me, no doubt taking in the sight of the oversized robe and my sleep-tousled hair. He'd seen me looking worse, but I couldn't help feeling self-conscious. Not that I'd given it any serious thought, but I supposed if I ever saw him again, I wanted him to see me looking happy, confident and, above all, sexy. That wasn't quite the vibe I gave off at this moment, if his expression was any indication.

'Hey, Lily.' Alex smiled broadly. I did my best to rearrange my features into the same expression, but curiosity and anger made that hard.

'Alex. This is a surprise …' So many questions crowded

my mind, all demanding urgent answers.

'Well, aren't you going to invite me in?'

'Oh, of course. Where are my manners? Come through.'

I ushered him into the kitchen, told him to sit down at the table and put the kettle on. As I waited for it to boil, I put food down for Dexter, who snuffled gratefully into his bowl.

Even after all this time, I remembered just how Alex liked his tea; strong, with just a dash of milk. I poured a mug, then a second, milkier one for myself.

'So …' I passed the mug of tea to him, marvelling how much at ease he looked. I didn't know how to begin phrasing everything I wanted to ask. My world had already been turned on its axis by the passionate night I'd spent with Ryan. Now here was Alex, shaking everything up again.

'Yeah, I guess you must be wondering why I'm here. Well, it's a bit of a complicated story, but you know I moved to that place in Dalston after you and I …?' He didn't need to finish the sentence. 'Well, I'm moving again. I exchanged contracts on a flat in a new development near the Olympic stadium site a couple of days ago.'

'Oh, Alex, that's great news. Though I don't see quite what it has to do with me.'

He blew on his tea before taking a sip. 'I've been going through a lot of stuff I had in storage, seeing how much of it I actually need, you know? And I found an old photo album in amongst all the clutter. There were snaps of you and me on that holiday in Rome, in that little trattoria near the Palazzo Venezia, remember? And some from that party Mick and Elaine threw, where everyone had to come dressed as fairies …'

'Yes, that was quite an evening – what I recall of it.' How had we reached the stage where we were making small talk, reminiscing about the old days and the mutual friends we'd had? I needed to be firm with him. 'But it still doesn't explain why you're in Dorset, or how you found me.'

'Look, I'll be straight with you, Lily. I looked at all those photos, and saw how happy we were together, and I started to realise what a stupid, stupid mistake I made in letting you go.'

I didn't know what to say. Fortunately, Ryan distracted me from having to respond by popping his head round the kitchen door.

'Hey, Lily, everything OK?'

'Yeah, I'm fine. Ryan, you remember Alex Baines, don't you?'

Ryan walked in, and I noticed he'd dressed in T-shirt and shorts, giving no clue to the fact he'd just got out of bed – a bed I'd been sharing, at that. He gave Alex an appraising glance, as though sizing up the competition. 'Of course. You came down to stay the weekend here with Lily, and you had that wicked sports car.'

'Still do,' Alex replied.

'There's tea in the pot if you want some, Ryan,' I told him. For one surreal moment, I thought that once he'd poured himself a mug, he'd come and join us at the kitchen table, adding an extra level of weirdness to the situation.

Instead, he said, 'I'm going to wander down to the beach. I've had a few texts from people telling me what a great time they had last night, but I think I ought to go and see how much clearing up needs to be done.'

'OK,' I replied. 'Give me a shout if you need anything.' Turning back to Alex, I explained, 'Ryan's been staying here for a few weeks. He and his friends threw a party on the beach last night. It was quite a bash. Never thought I'd ever find myself dancing to drum-and-bass classics on the sand ...' I knew I was babbling, but Alex's presence continued to throw me.

'Sounds like things are going well for you,' Alex commented.

Maybe last night went well, I wanted to tell him, but you don't have a clue what's happened since you walked out on me. You reduce me to a state where I can't even write a coherent sentence any more, then you breeze back into my life like you've never been away.

'Like I said,' he continued, taking my silence for agreement, 'I've been thinking about us, and I know now I should never have left. What we had – it wasn't over, not by a long way. I was foolish to think it was. And I knew I was prepared to do whatever it took to win you back. So I went round to your flat. Except, of course, you weren't there any more. But the girl who lives there now gave me your forwarding address. Of course, I recognised it from having been here before. I rang your mobile to warn you I was coming, but your voicemail kept picking up, so – well, I thought I'd surprise you.'

And you did that all right, I thought. Though I couldn't help noticing he'd kept my number – just as I'd kept his, even though I told myself repeatedly I should delete it. Maybe the bond between us was still a little tighter than either of us had cared to admit, till now.

For the first time since Alex had turned up unannounced on the doorstep, I regarded him properly. I had to admit he looked good; he'd cut his hair shorter than it had been at any point when we'd been together, but it suited him, and his hazel eyes still held the twinkle that had always captivated me.

'Yeah, I had the phone switched off,' I lied. If I'd been sleeping in my own bed, I'd have heard it ringing. And if I'd answered it, what would I have said? Would I have told Alex I wasn't interested in whatever he had to say, or would I have weakened and told him I'd be happy to see him again?

Alex drained the last of his tea, rose to put the empty mug in the sink. 'So what I came here to say, Lily, is that I miss you, more than I ever thought I would. I need you. And I want you back in my life.'

'Stop right there, Alex.' Stunned, I struggled to keep my composure. I got to my feet, wanting to be on an even footing with him. 'You walk out on me, without any real explanation. You let months go by, and then you just turn up and tell me it's all been a mistake and you want us to go back to how things were before. Are you serious?'

'I've never been more so ...' He pulled me into an embrace, stroking a stray curl out of my eyes. He smelled of the woody cologne I'd loved so much I'd bought him bottles of it for Christmas, and I sank a little deeper into his arms as all the old, familiar feelings washed over me. Alex was right; we'd shared so much together. We knew each other so well, were perfectly accepting of each other's little foibles and failings. The chance to get all that back again was incredibly tempting.

'I know this is a lot for you to take in, but I'm completely sincere,' Alex assured me. 'Say you'll have me back.'

The back door swung open, distracting me from answering him. Ryan strode in, to be greeted by the sight of Alex holding me tight, a moment of apparent tenderness passing between us. The hurt in his eyes was impossible to ignore, and my heart gave a lurch, as though it was trying to break out of my chest. I realised in that moment which of the two I really wanted to be with, and the knowledge gave me the impetus to break out of Alex's clasp.

'OK, I know what's going on here,' Ryan said, 'and I know when I'm not wanted. I think it's better if I'm not around for a while.' With that, he turned on his heel and fled, stumbling through the garden towards the cliff path.

I flew to the door, calling, 'Ryan, Ryan, wait! I can explain.' He didn't look back; just kept running till he'd disappeared from view and the sound of his sneaker-clad feet no longer echoed on the garden path.

Alex caught hold of my shoulder. 'Don't tell me,' he said with a laugh. 'The guy's got some kind of crazy crush on you. It's all right. He'll get over it.'

I spun round, beating at his chest with my fists, angered at Alex's dismissal of Ryan's feelings for me as just a crush.

What we'd shared the night before went so much deeper than that. 'No, it's not all right. I've got to go after him.'

'Dressed like that?' Alex snorted. 'Don't be ridiculous, Lily.'

'OK, so I'll go and change, and then I'll find Ryan. And when we come back here, I'd appreciate it if you weren't around.'

Now it was Alex's turn to question whether I was serious. 'You'd really choose him over me?' he asked incredulously.

'Every time,' I replied. 'I'm sorry, Alex. I can't go back to you.'

The laundry basket, piled high with clothes I'd washed the day before, waited at the bottom of the stairs. Neither Ryan nor I had found the time to take it upstairs in all the excitement surrounding the party. I plucked the first garment that came to hand from the pile, a short, floaty blue sundress. Not caring that Alex might be peeking round the kitchen door, I let the robe drop to the ground, and pulled the dress over my head. I didn't bother with any underwear, just stepped into a pair of flat sandals, grabbed my door key and left the house without a backward glance.

Not wanting to pass Alex again, I used the front door. It meant doubling back on myself, taking the little rutted track between Amanda's cottage and its neighbour to get down to the edge of the cliff. Slithering and sliding on loose scree, I scrambled my way down the cliff path. At the bottom, I looked left and right, trying to get any clues as to which way Ryan had gone, but the sand was churned up with dozens of sets of footprints left behind by the partygoers. Ryan could have walked on this exact spot, and I wouldn't be any the wiser. Looking at the blackened remnants of the pit where the barbecue had stood, I blinked back tears. Last night, everything had been perfect. Now Alex's unexpected appearance – and my reaction to it – had ruined everything.

Calling Ryan's name brought no response. Taking a

moment to get my phone and bring it with me would have made sense; there was no guarantee he'd have answered it if he'd seen I was calling, but I might have been able to get hold of Giles or Charlie, see if they could knock some sense into him. I needed to speak to a sympathetic voice right now.

Short of options, I started running along the sand, hoping to find some trace of Ryan's steps. On any other day, I'd have welcomed the fact the beach was deserted, but now a friendly passer-by might just have been able to tell me whether they'd seen a blond man heading in their direction. Every few hundred yards, I paused to look round, shouting, 'Ryan! Ryan, where are you?' until my voice was hoarse. My footwear wasn't really suitable for running any kind of distance, and it wasn't long before blisters had formed on both my heels. I could no longer see the little row of cottages on the cliff top, and realised I must have covered the best part of two miles in my futile search for Ryan.

Admitting defeat, I slipped the sandals off and went down to the water's edge to bathe my sore feet, making no attempt to stem the tears that flowed down my cheeks. Ryan would come back home in his own time; I'd have to deal with the consequences when he did.

Some instinct told me to look back in the direction I'd come, and that's when I saw him walking toward me.

'Lily? Lily, are you OK?' he asked. 'What are you doing here? Shouldn't you be back with Alex?'

I shook my head. 'I came looking for you. I wanted to explain everything.'

'What's to explain?' he asked. 'I saw the two of you together and you looked pretty cosy. It seemed as soon as you saw him again, what happened last night didn't mean anything.'

'That's not true,' I retorted. 'It meant more than you know. Yes, Alex wanted me to get back together with him, but I had the choice – and I didn't take it. I chose you,

Ryan.'

He looked at me as though he didn't quite believe what I was telling him. 'Really?'

'Really. Oh, I'm not denying that it felt good to be back in Alex's arms, and I thought if I went with you, it'd be too much of a risk. I'd be letting my heart rule my head. But then I realised that's what I want. When Alex walked out, he left me in a state where I couldn't even write any more, and part of me knows that if he did that once, who's to say he won't do it again?'

'But you looked right together,' Ryan said. 'You can't deny that.'

'Well, I caught sight of us in the mirror in your bedroom last night, and I thought we looked pretty good together too. I'm not stupid, Ryan. I know there's no guarantee we have any more of a future together than I would with Alex, and I know the age difference between us might be an issue – if not for us, then for people like your mother – but I'm already falling in love with you, and I'm willing to take a chance on this working out if you are.'

It was a declaration any of the heroines in my book would have been proud of, and I meant every word of it. At first, Ryan didn't respond, and I worried that our relationship was over before it had even really begun. Then he took me in his arms, crushing my breasts against his hard chest, and kissed me with a passion that left my lips swollen and pouting.

'Oh, Lily.' He sighed. 'There's nothing I want more.'

Hand in hand, we took the walk back to the cottage at a slow pace, Ryan mindful of my blistered feet. There was no sign of Alex when we arrived; his car had gone, and he hadn't left as much as a goodbye note. I doubted I'd ever see him again and, despite everything that had happened, I couldn't help feeling a pang of sadness at the way things had ended.

'This will sound crazy,' I said, half to myself, 'but I can't help wishing we'd parted on better terms.'

'Don't worry about him any more,' Ryan said. 'Let's go upstairs and I'll treat you to a foot massage.'

Barefoot, I let Ryan lead me upstairs. While I made myself comfortable on my bed, he went to the bathroom and filled a bowl with warm water. Using lavender-scented soap and a flannel, he carefully washed my feet clean of the sand and saltwater that crusted their soles, before rubbing them with soothing aloe vera lotion. His touch was sure, avoiding the sorest places, and I gave in to the sheer pleasure of having my feet so expertly massaged.

'You're very good at this,' I murmured, as the pads of Ryan's thumbs worked at the ball of my foot, just below my big toe, sending thrills all the way up to my pussy.

'Sh, just lie back and enjoy it,' he instructed me. When his lotion-slick hands slowly, surely moved higher, up my shins and heading for my thighs, I didn't object. It had been a very long time since I'd had anyone concentrate on giving me pleasure with such single-minded purpose, and I wanted to enjoy every last moment of it. Without thinking, I adjusted my position on the bed, letting my legs loll apart a little more.

'Oh fuck,' I heard Ryan murmur, his gaze concentrated on the view up my skirt. 'You're not wearing any knickers.'

'I – er – didn't have time to put any on,' I admitted. 'I did leave the house in a bit of a hurry.'

'Well, if you ever feel like forgetting them in future, don't let me stop you,' he replied. Using the flats of his hands, he pushed my thighs further apart, staring at the intricate whorls of my sex and breathing in my sharp, excited scent. 'Oh Lily, I've just got to taste you.'

With that, he bent close, flicking out his tongue so he could run it the length of my cleft. My breath hissed in my throat as he made contact with the wet, sensitive flesh. Heartened by my reaction, he began to lick and lap in earnest, exploring all the way from the tight nub of my clit to the dark, hidden pucker of my anal hole. When the flat of his tongue brushed over that most intimate place, I wriggled with guilty delight.

'You like that, don't you, you bad girl?' Ryan chuckled. 'God, I'm going to have so much fun finding out all your naughty secrets.'

'Just as long as I get to find out yours,' I replied, though I already reckoned I could get him hard in his underwear any time I chose to let him know I wasn't wearing any panties. Because of his crouched-over position, I couldn't see his crotch, but I knew he'd be hard now, cock stimulated beyond belief by the sight and taste of my bare, juicy pussy.

As he continued to tease me, taking each of my inner lips in his mouth in turn and sucking gently on them, I played with my aching nipples through my dress, pinching and squeezing them. My breasts felt full, swollen with desire, and if I hadn't been enjoying the feel of Ryan's mouth on my sex so much, I'd have wanted him to suckle at them.

'Let's get you naked,' Ryan said, breaking off from what he was doing so he could guide me into a sitting position. He pulled the dress off over my head, before rapidly stripping out of his own clothes. Just as I'd suspected, his cock stood at full mast, the thick, rigid pole bobbing with his movements.

Naked and aroused, Ryan got back on the bed, lifting my legs over his shoulders so he could really bury his head in my pussy, his tongue laving my clit while his index finger burrowed up into my hole. That combination of finger and tongue stimulated me just where I needed it. Even before I was aware of it, my thigh muscles were gripping Ryan's head, keeping it in place while I bucked against his mouth, sobbing and gasping with the force of my climax.

When I released my hold on him, his chin was iced with my juices and he was grinning broadly. 'Wow, I've never made anyone come so hard before!'

'Hopefully that's only the start,' I replied, 'but I think we need to do something about this ...'

Reaching out a hand, I wrapped my fingers round the plump head of his cock, stroking lightly but with definite intent. Ryan's breathing quickened as I toyed with him.

'Should I go get a condom or two?' he panted.

I shook my head. 'That might not be necessary. Just let me check first.'

My handbag lay on the floor, close to the bed. Hunting through it, past the usual litter of lipsticks, tampons, ballpoint pens, and packets of tissues, I finally found what I'd been looking for: a discreet black condom case. Opening it up, I found a strip of three condoms. If I remembered rightly, I'd bought them only a couple of days before Alex and I had split up, never dreaming we wouldn't get to use them. They'd lain forgotten in the depths of my bag, until now.

Ryan quickly rolled one into place, then came to lie beside me on the bed. I was struck with the urge to be on top, and he didn't complain when I pushed him down on his back, throwing a leg over his broad thighs. We kissed, hot and eager, as I held his cock, brushing it with my pussy lips a couple of times until he was begging me to stop teasing him.

With that, I inched myself down, my eyes never leaving his, feeling my muscles ripple and contract around the thick, latex-coated length of him. Just as before, I marvelled at the way he fitted so nicely inside me, almost as if he'd been designed to my exact specifications.

As soon as I began to move, I knew the orgasm I'd experienced earlier had only been the curtain-raiser. Sensation sparked in my belly, like little fireworks fizzing and bursting, letting me know the main event was about to take place.

Ryan nuzzled each of my nipples in turn, gently biting the little buds and making me squeal with delight. I rode him faster, rising and falling with increasing purpose. His hands gripped my bum cheeks, and as we both got closer to coming, he lifted me up and down on his shaft.

'Yes, that's it,' I cried out, lost in a world where there was room for nothing but the steady pressure of my crotch rubbing against Ryan's, the wiry hair around the root of his cock tickling my soft skin. The ripples that preceded the storm waves of orgasm spread out from my clit, and I let them carry me away. Beneath me, Ryan groaned, thrusting up hard at me as his own orgasm hit him, and I closed my eyes, speaking words that didn't make any sense as I came like I never had before.

It was a long time before either of us could do anything more than gasp for breath and cling on tight to each other. At last, Ryan's hold on me relaxed and I climbed off his groin, giddy and sated with pleasure.

'Now do you doubt that I made the right choice?' I asked, as we cuddled close.

He shook his head. 'You know what you said earlier, about falling in love? Well, you make it so easy to do, Lily.

With that, he kissed me again and I knew that, no matter what else came of my long hot summer's house-sitting for Amanda, I'd always have this beautiful, unforgettable moment to look back on. And many more to come, I hoped.

Epilogue

'YOU MAKE IT SO *easy to fall in love.*'

I looked at the words again, before typing *"THE END"* beneath them. All writers are magpies, always listening out for the perfect line that they can borrow for their own purposes, and that's what I'd tell Ryan if he ever saw his heartfelt declaration spilling from the lips of the hero of *Seafront Attraction*. It was more than a possibility, given that he'd worked his way through all my other published novels; if he did, he'd also discover I'd dedicated this latest book to him, with all my love.

Time for a celebratory coffee, I thought, or maybe something a little stronger. Maybe I'd see if Ryan and the boys wanted to join me in a glass of the Prosecco I'd put in the fridge, ready for the moment when I finished the last line of my manuscript. They were down the landing in Ryan's room, listening to some Nu-metal band or other, the thump-thump of the bass audible even through the closed door. I didn't worry about it; I'd been in the zone for the last week or so, tearing through the remaining chapters of the novel and wondering how I'd ever had a problem finishing it. They could have had an entire stack of speakers blasting out music day and night and it wouldn't have disturbed me.

Later, when Giles and Charlie had gone back to their bed and breakfast accommodation for the evening, Ryan and I could have a more intimate celebration of our own. We'd waited a couple of days before admitting to them that we were sleeping with each other; their reaction had been to roll their eyes and wonder what had taken us so long. I had the feeling Amanda wouldn't be quite so sanguine when she found out, but I'd worry about that when it happened. Everything between Ryan and me was still so new, I was trying to take everything as slowly as I could, though the overwhelming passion we felt for each other sometimes made that hard.

I knew that, unlike the heroines of my novels, I wasn't guaranteed a happy-ever-after ending. But this had the potential to be much more than just a summer fling. Looking into Ryan's eyes as I invited the boys to come down and join me in a drink, seeing the depth of emotion reflected there, I had the feeling we'd be heating up the winter too.

Heating Up Winter. Now, there's a title for a novel, I thought, mentally filing it away till I was back at my computer. I'd recovered my writing touch, I'd found my perfect lover and I couldn't be happier. Ryan's footsteps close on the stairs behind me, his friends whooping their congratulations at me as they followed in his wake, I went to open the Prosecco.

Just Another Lady
by Penelope Friday

Chapter One

ELINOR EVERTON COULD DATE almost to the day when it was that she had begun to fall in love with Lucius Crozier. It was a hot summer, and Lucius had come home from Harrow, suddenly grown up and unexpectedly handsome, no longer the schoolboy with whom the tomboy Elinor had loved to squabble. The Croziers had come, *en famille*, to see the Evertons; and Elinor had tumbled into the room to greet Lucius with her usual informality, only to be shocked into shyness and embarrassment at this new version of her old companion. Suddenly her limbs all seemed too long; her red hair shamefully in need of brushing; her dress grubby and unflattering.

'Good morning, Elinor,' said Lucius, his voice a deep drawl.

Elinor felt something flutter inside her. Lucius had never made her feel this way before. 'H ... hello,' she stammered, standing on one leg and then the other, shifting her weight uncomfortably.

There was an expression on Lucius's face which made Elinor feel as if he were laughing at her, which only increased her discomfort.

Her father said, 'The girl doesn't recognise you, Lucius,' in a cheerful teasing manner, and Elinor felt herself blush.

'How are you?' she asked, her voice small.

Lucius leaned back in his chair and flicked an imaginary piece of fluff from his impeccable waistcoat. 'All the better for seeing you, Elinor, of course.'

Elinor bit her lip, sure she was being teased, not quite certain whether she liked or loathed it. Certainly it gave her a funny feeling that she could not quite process. That feeling had grown as she and Lucius had been thrown into each other's company over the next few weeks. Sometimes he seemed to treat her like a little girl; at other moments, he would look at her in a strange way, or make a comment which seemed to hint at something more than the mild affection of a young gentleman for a tearaway girl barely out of her childhood. Every day she fell further and further in love; a feeling which she resented and was frightened of – for why would Lucius Crozier ever take an interest in her, a girl with unladylike manners, unruly auburn hair and no expectations to speak of?

She attempted to make up for this by baiting Lucius as much as she could: if he said the day was fine, she would say it was "too hot". If he had told her black was black, she would have said it was white. Their squabbles became regular and more and more venomous, until one day Lucius grabbed her wrist and pulled her to face him.

'What is the matter with you, Elinor Everton?' he demanded.

She'd have had to look up to meet his gaze, so she stared firmly at his shoulder. The place where his fingers touched her wrist felt hot and strange; she was aware of her senses prickling.

'Surely I am allowed to disagree with you sometimes?' she demanded, aware she sounded petulant. 'Just because The Great Lucius Crozier says something is true, that does not make it infallible.'

'Elinor … Damn it! Look at me, won't you?'

'No.'

He put his other hand under her chin and forced it up so

that their eyes locked. Elinor found it hard to breathe properly; she was not sure whether she wanted to run away or fling herself into his arms.

'What is the matter with both of us?' he murmured quietly.

She felt his gaze rest on her mouth, and her lips tingled in response. He was going to kiss her – was he? Did she want him to? Before either of them could move further, Elinor's mother came into view. Elinor wrenched herself out of Lucius's grip.

'Get off me, you wretch,' she said fiercely. 'I hate you.'

She had taken a few steps away before she heard Lucius's response. 'The feeling,' he called after her, 'is most certainly mutual.'

After that, it was war to the knife between the pair.

Nevertheless, those days seemed a long time ago now.

They dated before Lucius gained his reputation as a womaniser and gambler. Before the death of Elinor's father Augustus; before the terms attached to the family entail had pushed Elinor and her mother in one fell swoop from riches to barely surviving in genteel poverty. Before their situation had deteriorated further with the serious illness which now racked her mother. Elinor and Lucius moved in very different circles now; very different indeed.

Which was why the announcement by their maid (their one and *only* maid) that Mr Crozier was requesting to speak to Elinor came as rather a shock.

'Thank you, Molly,' she said quietly. 'Please assure him I will be down presently.'

'Yes, Miss.'

The maid withdrew. Elinor could see a glint of interest in Molly's eyes, and could not blame her. Elinor too was wondering why Lucius should visit unexpectedly like this. Their challenging relationship, with each liking to get the last word in any discussion or dispute, had hardly hinted at surprise visits in later days. Perhaps, she thought wryly, Lucius was here to get the very last word: to rub in finally the gulf between their separate positions. Even without this morning's final blow of a doctor's bill Elinor knew she could not pay, their circumstances were now like chalk and cheese. He was owed, Elinor admitted privately, his victory.

She was never going to give him that satisfaction, however. Elinor Everton would keep her stubborn pride to the end. Smoothing her dress down, and hoping that the many darns were not over-evident, she took a quick look in the dusty mirror at her hair (still tightly coiled) and descended the shabbily carpeted stairs to the withdrawing room.

'Mr Crozier.' Her smile was rather forced, but the best she could produce. She gave a brief curtsey, and he bowed in return.

'Miss Everton,' he replied. 'How formal we are today.'

Elinor thought fleetingly of the days in which they had been Elinor and Lucius to one another, and dismissed the pang of regret for what had gone.

'What can I do for you?' she asked.

'It is more a case,' said Lucius, 'of what I can do for you.'

'I fail to understand.'

Lucius glanced at the sofa. 'May I ...'

'Please, be seated,' Elinor said coldly, placing herself on the edge of a chair as far from him as possible.

'Thank you.' Lucius settled himself with his usual elegance. 'You are as beautiful as ever, Elinor.'

Elinor did not dignify this with a response; instead she kept her green eyes firmly on his face, waiting for him to come to the point.

He laughed. 'You are also, as ever, impossible to distract with compliments.'

'If you consider your words to be such. For my sake, I prefer to be admired rather for my abilities than my looks.'

This was not quite true: Elinor was human, was female, enough to be flattered by Lucius's words. But that was something she was certainly not prepared to acknowledge aloud.

'You are also,' said Lucius, his mien unchanged by Elinor's sharp retort, 'regrettably short of money.'

Elinor felt her whole body tense at his words. The Evertons' parlous financial state was no doubt evident to all, but she was grateful that most people did not feel authorised to comment aloud on it. 'We manage,' she said tightly.

'Do you? I had heard otherwise.' He shrugged. 'Lack of funds is fortunately not a situation I am personally acquainted with, but I gather that you –'

Elinor interrupted him before he could make any further remark; insult her further. 'I do not want your money.' Her breast heaved with short angry breaths. Had Lucius come here to offer patronage? She stood up and began to pace back and forth, aware all the time of Lucius's eyes on her.

'No?' Lucius raised an eyebrow. 'What *do* you want from me, then, Elinor Everton?'

'Nothing,' she lied.

Once, she had thought that perhaps ...

But that had been a long time ago. She looked at him and knew she still wanted him, and the thought hurt. Too many issues now lay in their way: complicated things like Pride, and Money, and Power. Lucius had all three; what Elinor lacked in the last two, she made up in spades with the first.

'I, you see,' explained Lucius, as if the small passage between them had not occurred, 'am plentifully supplied with the oh-so-filthy lucre on which our world turns, but regrettably lacking a wife.'

'I never heard that you considered that much of a misfortune,' Elinor shot back.

'No?' Lucius smiled. 'I never realised you kept yourself so acquainted with the minutiae of my life. I am flattered that you cared to do so.' Elinor felt herself blushing; knew that Lucius could see the tell-tale colour flooding to her cheeks. He allowed the silence to linger for a moment before continuing to speak. 'Nevertheless, there you have it. I am in need of a – shall we say – an *amenable* wife; you are in need of money. It seems we both have something the other requires.'

Elinor stopped pacing and stood looking down at Lucius. 'Do you really think,' she asked, her voice low, 'that I would sell myself for my own betterment?'

Lucius's answer was oblique. 'I gather your mother's doctor's bills are large.'

'I'll manage something.' Elinor dug her fingernails deeply into her palms. She couldn't bring herself to say that she didn't need money. She needed it so desperately it hurt. Mrs Everton's chances of recovery were minimal without the continued attendance of the doctor.

A doctor who would not be returning unless his last bill was paid.

If the money had been for herself, it would have been easy to refuse Lucius. But for her mother – oh, for her mother ... And in one way, it was so tempting to take up his offer. After all, it was not as if he were suggesting something she did not want to do. Elinor thought about the offers she had refused in her first season, and faced for the first time the knowledge that it had been thoughts of Lucius which had prevented her marrying before. But that had been when things were different. When she was a decent match for an eligible young man.

To drop her pride, though, to the extent that she would marry Lucius in order to let him pay her family's debts for her? It was too much to ask. Too much. In an unusual moment of self-doubt, Elinor wondered whether the only reason Lucius had made the offer was because he knew she wouldn't take it. He could humiliate her with no fear of reprisals – no fear of finding himself saddled with an unwanted wife. It was not as if by birth she was no match for Lucius. But since her father's unexpected early death, Elinor and her mother had moved ever further down the social ladder. Now they owned nothing, not even a house; and Elinor's mother was sick.

'Of course, I would require an obedient wife,' Lucius said.

'Then it is fortunate that I do not aspire to the position,' Elinor replied through gritted teeth.

Lucius smiled. 'Three days, Elinor. Tell me your answer then.'

There must be something. There had to be something. Elinor thought she would rather die than marry Lucius for his money. She spent three days trying every possible avenue – governessing, even chamber-maid positions; but it was made clear to her that she was not considered an appropriate candidate for either. Too ill-educated for the first; too well-educated for the second.

And meantime she watched her mother dying, inch by inevitable inch.

Lucius came on the third day, and she arrayed herself in her best – or rather, in her least worn – dress to meet him. When Molly announced his arrival, Elinor forced herself to look at him, to make the expected curtsey. And then to say, her eyes lowered in shame, that she would marry him.

'I accept your proposal. And I thank you for it.' The second sentence caused bile to rise in her mouth, but it had to be done. He had bought and paid for her; her future now was to be the dutiful, *obedient*, wife which he required.

'I am overcome by the honour.'

Elinor wanted to kill him for the mocking tone in which the words were drawled. Instead, she said, 'When?' Her voice was strained. 'I mean ...'

'You can hardly wait for the day.'

'I need ...'

'Of course.' Lucius's tone was dry. 'You need my

77

money. Rest assured, Miss Everton, that from the moment at which our betrothal is announced in the press – tonight, if you wish – your creditors will no longer be knocking upon your door. On the contrary, you will find yourself buried under a deluge of well-wishers and those who wish to sell you fripperies for this miraculous wedding.'

'I feel sure I will be the envy of the débutantes,' said Elinor, hating the fact that it was true; that she was certainly not the only lady who had looked upon Lucius and desired him. Hating that she could offer him nothing, and he had everything. Nothing? Well, only one thing. Her body. Perhaps it would be less shameful to be a whore out and out; to act a little on the stage, and then act more behind the scenes with man after faceless man. But that would have killed her mother as surely as the illness would do without treatment. Selling herself, body and soul, to this one man was the only acceptable option she had.

The honeymoon, such as it would be, was going to entail 14 nights at Redvers, Lucius's country house, so that Elinor could assure herself of her mother's improved health. After that ...

'London?' Elinor demanded, shocked.

'It *is* where I live, at any rate during the season,' Lucius explained, mock apologetically.

London. Of course, Elinor should have realised that Lucius was hardly the archetypal country gentleman. Had known it, in fact. But – it had never occurred to her that her main residence would be anywhere but her home village of Carryleigh. Certainly she had had her London season, several years back; but that had always been, in her mind, a once in a lifetime occasion, an anomaly. It was not that she had not fitted in, nor even that she had not enjoyed herself, but it was not *life*. Not life as Elinor had always envisaged it, anyway.

But then so much of life was not turning out as Elinor had imagined.

'London,' she said again, resignedly. 'Of course. And mother?'

Lucius's expression was unreadable, but his words were plain enough. 'I hardly think she will be ready for the exigencies of London life,' he said gently. 'I thought – Rocklands?' Rocklands was a cottage on the edge of Lucius's estate, considerably larger than the Evertons' current establishment, not to mention a great deal more comfortable. 'A couple of maids; a companion, if she wished?'

He was burying her in generosity, Elinor thought helplessly. Coals of fire on her head. And what did she have to offer him in return?

'Thank you,' she said quietly. 'Mother would love that, I know.'

'And you?'

All she had to offer was acquiescence. 'Of course. It sounds delightful.'

'And I may kiss my bride-to-be?'

Elinor felt her heart beat harder, faster; felt as if a small flame was burning inside her. For the first time in years, she was suddenly reminded of that hot summer day when she had thought, for a few exciting seconds, that Lucius might kiss her. 'Yes,' she whispered.

Lucius moved across to her, and took her hands in his, smoothing his thumbs over her palms. Her skin tingled where he touched. He pulled her in towards him, close enough that Elinor could feel his warm breath against her cheek. She realised she was trembling slightly, and hoped that Lucius would not notice.

'And now,' Lucius murmured, 'I do this ...'

He took one of his hands from hers, and cupped it around her cheek, tilting her face towards his. For the first time in their relationship, Elinor found herself too shy to meet his eyes, and she shut hers. She had a strange urge to press herself closer to him, so that their bodies melded together;

but before she could do so, he had bent his head and pressed warm, masculine lips to hers. They clung to the contours of her mouth for a second before he let go, stepping away. Elinor blinked, and opened her eyes, shaken by her reaction to the kiss.

The kiss. A kiss. Elinor had been kissed for the first time, and by Lucius Crozier. A faint blush spread over her cheeks, and she turned away to prevent Lucius from seeing it. It took her a couple of seconds to compose herself, then she spoke. 'That ... that was ...' She paused, uncertain of what word to use to describe the experience. 'Nice,' she offered.

'You flatter me,' Lucius said dryly.

'I mean ...' But Elinor sighed and did not finish the sentence. She did not have the vocabulary for what had happened. 'Never mind.'

'Indeed.' Lucius changed the subject. 'Well, I have your consent for your marriage, but I believe it is traditional to get the consent of a lady's parent to her betrothal. Usually, of course, it is the father, but in the present circumstances – perhaps I could have a private word with Mrs Everton?'

'No.' The word came out more sharply than Elinor had intended. 'It's not – I mean – she isn't well. She isn't receiving.' The clichéd words slid off her tongue.

'Are you ashamed of me, Elinor?'

'Of course I am not.'

It was not, after all, Lucius of whom Elinor was ashamed, but herself. It would kill her mother – almost certainly literally – to know that her daughter had sold herself in order to acquire medical care for her. Not that Lucius would be as crass as to say, nor even imply, any such thing, of course, but Elinor felt that this was one conversation best dealt with herself. More objections followed thick and fast in her mind: she could not bear to think of Lucius seeing the state of any other room in her house, and most particularly the one bedroom which she and her mother shared. Nor could she stand and listen to Lucius give fallacious reasons for his offer of marriage: nothing but a conviction that he loved Elinor dearly would allow Mrs Everton to agree to their wedding, and Elinor suspected that the very sight of this smart, handsome gentleman alongside impoverished Elinor Everton would make it obvious that this could not be a marriage of love. King Cophetua and the Beggar Maid was but a story, after all. How Elinor herself would deal with the conversation, she did not know; that, however, could wait for another time.

'Please,' she said quietly. 'Let me do it.'

He bowed ironically. 'Your wish is my command, of course.'

He left without kissing her again. Elinor couldn't help but see this as an omen.

The bedroom was small and dark, and there was mould on one of the walls. Elinor cleaned it off regularly, but as regularly it grew back. Her mother lay in bed, the pallor of her skin evident in the dark room. Elinor felt her heart contract as she looked at her.

'Mamma,' she said quietly.

Mrs Everton's face was lined with pain, but she summoned up a smile for her daughter. 'Hello, darling.'

Elinor crossed the room, and sat on the side of the bed, taking one of her mother's claw-like hands in her own.

'Mamma, I have something to tell you.' She saw her mother's face contract.

'Bills?' her mother said wearily.

'No, not this time.' Elinor forced a smile on to her face. 'Something a lot nicer than bills, dear. In fact …' She took a big breath. '… I've got some rather exciting news.'

She was rewarded by the look of interest which took years off her mother. For a second, Elinor could see the young vibrant Mamma of her youth.

'Tell me, then,' Mrs Everton encouraged.

Elinor swallowed. She had practised the lines time

enough before coming up to speak to her mother, but somehow the words wouldn't form with the ease they had when she had not had her mother's wan face in front of her. All the practised sentences fled from her.

'I'm getting married,' she said bluntly.

The expressions which crossed her mother's face were indescribable. Hope, suspicion, worry, interest …

'I don't understand.' Mrs Everton's hand tightened on Elinor. 'How can you? To whom? Oh – *not* the doctor!' – this last in a voice of woe.

Of all the responses Elinor had expected, this was the last, and she actually laughed out loud. 'Mamma! How can you?'

A fit of giggles overtook her, and her mother joined in. For several minutes their laughter rang round the room, and Elinor thought that if her prospective marriage did nothing else, it had been worth it for this moment alone. Finally, when they calmed down a little, her mother spoke.

'Well, if it isn't the doctor – and frankly, my dear, we hardly see any other gentleman for you to become engaged to – who is it?'

Elinor took a deep breath. 'Lucius Crozier.'

The lines of worry returned around her mother's face. 'Darling …'

Elinor interrupted her hastily, her words flowing out, she hoped convincingly. 'Yes, Mamma – isn't it wonderful? He came round … I mean … Well, you know we've always been close, and–'

It was her mother's turn to interrupt. 'I know you've always argued,' she said dubiously.

'I've always wanted him.' There was a desperate truth in Elinor's words. She'd wanted him to be around when she was younger; later, she had wanted something very, very different from him. The memory of today's kiss still lingered in her breasts, in a dampness between her legs. She didn't know precisely what she wanted of Lucius, but she knew she wanted more.

'Then I am happy for you.'

Elinor watched the worry lines fade once more. The honesty of what she said had been what swayed her mother; at the same time, she was glad Lucius had not been present to hear her. This was to be a marriage of convenience – for him! – and the least suggestion that she would hang around him like a wayward puppy seeking attention would send him running in the opposite direction.

Nevertheless, she woke in the middle of the night, sweaty and throbbing, thinking of Lucius.

Chapter Two

IT WAS HER WEDDING day. Elinor wasn't certain what one was supposed to feel on one's wedding day: perhaps the gnawing anxiety was normal. If so, it was the only thing which was normal about this day. It was hard to believe that in several hours time she would no longer be Miss Everton, but Mrs Crozier. Her heart leapt a bit at that thought, and she reminded herself severely that this was not a marriage of love, but of convenience. If she *had* to be in love with her husband-to-be, it was something to keep private. He did not want her love, and she could certainly do without the complications her feelings might bring in their wake.

She got up, and went over to the closet where her wedding dress hung. The beauty of the garment still made her gasp in disbelief that she might wear such a thing. It was white, with golden stitching decorating it. Elinor looked more ruefully at the underclothing: she was still not sure how she would ever manage to get dressed.

The morning passed in a blur. Lucius's money – Elinor would always think of it as "Lucius's" money, even when they were married, she thought – had paid for more servants; and Elinor and her mother were already living at Rocklands; a far cry from their previous home. There were plenty of people to bustle round, therefore, and Elinor was at the centre of the bustle at all times. She spent a bittersweet half hour sitting with her mother, whose health would not allow her to attend the wedding, to the great disappointment of them both. But the doctor's visits had become more regular, and Elinor could see traces of colour returning to her mother's cheeks. It was easy to feel certain that she had done the right thing in accepting Lucius's offer when she saw Mrs Everton's health improving daily. When she left her mother, however, time seemed to pass in a flash. She was to be "given away" by a cousin of Lucius's: not a usual proceeding, but the Evertons were remarkably short of family, and their recent poverty had made them, if not literally friendless, close to it. Elinor had played with Lucius's cousin on many an occasion in their youth; he was a gentle, sombre man – not exciting, perhaps, but reliable. Elinor had learned to rate reliability high over the last few years. So many "so-called" friends had melted away as the Evertons' finances dwindled; and in the last few years, Elinor had had more than her fair share of the "excitement" of not knowing where the next penny would come from.

So she found herself walking down the aisle towards Lucius. Her corset was tighter than anything she'd ever worn before; it rubbed against her breasts, making her nipples pointy and hard. There must have been perhaps fifty people in the church, but Elinor had eyes only for one: Lucius. He stood by the altar in a costume that looked as if it were moulded to his body, and for a second Elinor had to blink, trying not to think about what it was that his clothes were covering. The vicar spoke the first few words of the ceremony, and Elinor realised she was trembling, though whether with fear or excitement she was not sure. A short while later, she walked back up the aisle, Lucius at her side, with the knowledge that she was now, indeed, Mrs Crozier – Lucius's wife.

After a wedding "breakfast", where Elinor talked and laughed with an ever increasing sense of unreality, the guests began to disperse. Evening drew on, and it was not long before Elinor found herself alone, with her husband, in their (*their!* Elinor had never before thought that it was such a meaningful word) bedroom. Lucius smiled at her, and Elinor forced herself to smile in return; it was clearly not a great success, as he asked, 'Are you scared?'

'You would like to think so,' Elinor shot back, a little unfairly.

In all honesty, she was terrified. Lucius had already completed his part of the bargain: her mother was getting the best medical treatment there was. Elinor's part of the agreement was yet to come. Starting here, alone at night with a gentleman who would expect ... if truth be told, Elinor would have to admit that she did not quite know what it was that a gentleman expected of his bride. She knew how she'd felt when he'd kissed her: an almost uncomfortably tumultuous feeling in her stomach; a tightening of her nipples, a strange dampness between her legs. But kisses were one thing: what happened in a private bedroom between man and wife was something entirely different. And she did not know what it entailed.

'Undress for me, Elinor.' Lucius's voice was a tone lower than usual, the look in his eyes almost burning her with its heat.

'I ...' She felt her cheeks reddening with two separate emotions. 'I can't.'

'Oh, I think you'll find you can,' purred Lucius.

She bit her lip and glared at him, indignation winning over shyness. 'No, I mean I *can't*. I literally can't. This wretched corset is too damn tight for me to unfasten. It took two abigails to get me into the thing, and frankly I can't imagine that I'm ever going to be able to get it off.'

She saw Lucius's mouth quirk with amusement. 'I see. I will be happy to ... ah ... assist you when necessary.'

Elinor reminded herself, not for the first time, that obedient and dutiful wives did not tend to slap their new husband around the face. However tempting that might be.

'If you could unfasten the dress,' she said grimly, turning her back to him to present him with a row of small, creamy-white buttons.

The feel of Lucius's fingers running down her spine

made Elinor want to shiver. Even though she was protected by layers of clothing, the knowledge that he was stripping her – that shortly she would be naked in his company – made every touch tingle with what Elinor had to acknowledge to herself was excitement as much as embarrassment. As he unfastened the final button, she wriggled impatiently and the dress fell in a pool at her feet. The petticoat she could divest herself; the corset, however, needed Lucius's aid to remove. Elinor could feel his breath warm against her neck as he teasingly took his time to undo the strings. When at last it expanded around her, Elinor took what felt like the first decent breath since that morning, almost moaning her relief.

'You looked beautiful in it,' her husband (her *husband!*) murmured in her ear, 'but even more so out of it.'

He pushed it off her shoulders, so that she stood dressed only in the light cotton shift in front of him. As he turned her to face him, Elinor was suddenly made all too aware of her semi-nude state compared to Lucius's full dress. She could feel her nipples peaking against the cloth, almost begging for Lucius's touch.

'It's a little cold,' she said, taking a hasty step backwards and looking towards the huge bed. 'Um ... I think I'll ...'

'You want me to come to bed?' asked Lucius, smiling.

Do not show fear. Do not show fear. 'When you are ready to do so,' she said coolly.

'I am tempted to request that you perform the same task for me as I did for you,' Lucius said, 'and assist me with the removal of my clothing. But perhaps that can wait for another day.'

Another day. Elinor was reminded once more that this was life now; she was married to Lucius Crozier for the rest of her days. Up until that moment, she had been just thinking about getting through the wedding itself, and now the wedding night. But there would be tomorrow – and tomorrow – and tomorrow. Was it better or worse that she desired the man?

With that thought, she slipped towards the large double bed, shivering as her heated body came into contact with the cold sheets. Lucius had begun to strip, and Elinor was torn between shyness and a desperate wish to watch. Her eyes apparently discreetly lowered, she yet managed to gaze as he removed the first few layers of clothing. Suddenly she was finding it hard to breathe again. This time, she had no corset to blame for her state; but somehow the sight of Lucius's slim, muscular body was having a similarly constricting effect on her lungs. And then ...

'Oh,' she whispered, as Lucius stood naked before her, his manhood standing tall and proud and – 'It's so big.' Elinor couldn't drag her eyes away from it; it captured all of her attention. Were all men so – so well endowed, or was it just Lucius?

He strolled towards the bed. 'Do you like what you see?'

Elinor had no mind for anything but the truth. 'Yes.' Her fingers trembled as she reached out her hand towards his erection. 'May I?'

He had a half-smile on his face as he nodded. Elinor wasn't sure whether he was laughing at her, or merely pleased by her response. Almost she didn't care. She stroked his manhood with the very tips of her fingers, scared to damage him, to make something change, to make that beautiful jutting erection fade away in front of her.

He laughed. 'A little harder, Elinor; you tickle.'

She looked up at him from the bed. He looked happy, uncomplicatedly so. 'Like this?' She ran her fingers harder down his erection.

'Close your hand around me,' Lucius encouraged. He reached down and touched her breasts through the light shift she still wore. 'Like so.' He grasped one of her breasts from beneath, curling his fingers and thumb around it.

'Oh,' said Elinor again, wondering what magical connection there was between her breasts and the secret place between her thighs, as lightning-like shivers ran from one to the other and back again, making her feel as if a fire had been lit within her. She slid her fingers around his manhood, and ran her hand up and down tentatively.

'Mmm, like that,' he said approvingly.

'You're beautiful.' Elinor hadn't intended to say the words aloud, but they came out without volition.

'Sit up, Elinor of mine,' Lucius murmured. 'Let me help you off with that shift. Let me *see* you.'

Elinor's tongue circled her lips nervously. 'I – I'm not like you.'

Lucius laughed aloud. 'I hope not! Come.' He took his hand from her breast and hers from his erection, and Elinor almost moaned with disappointment. But he took her hands in his and pulled her to a sitting position. 'Now,' he instructed, 'wriggle out of that shift.'

Elinor could feel her cheeks burning hotly as she obeyed her husband. She knew she must disappoint. If even half of the rumours were true, Lucius had slept with much more beautiful ladies – and many of them. How could Elinor Everton ... Elinor *Crozier*, she reminded herself ... compete? Nevertheless, she pulled her shift over her head, her breasts exposed, and the cotton sheet now the only thing protecting her modesty below the waist. Lucius sat on the bed next to her, and she was aware of his eyes raking over her, but she could not look up to meet his eyes. He leaned down and kissed her gently on the lips, deepening the kiss as she responded to it. She felt his tongue touch hers, then plunge into the depths of her mouth. Her self-consciousness forgotten, she reached up to wrap her arms around him, kissing him back as fervently as she knew how.

Time stood still. The kiss might have taken seconds – minutes – longer still. Elinor did not know and she certainly did not care, so long as Lucius was with her, touching her, caressing her, kissing her. He pulled her over on the bed so that they were lying together on it. Her hand tangled in his hair; his hand reached once more for her breast, whilst he laid one possessive leg across her two. It felt amazing. It felt – right. Elinor wasn't scared any more, wasn't embarrassed. All she cared about was that this warmth, this fire burning through her, should continue.

'Please,' she said, burying her head into his neck and breathing in the unadulterated musky smell of Lucius Crozier. 'Please don't stop.'

'I don't intend to,' he assured her. 'Indeed, I thought I might...' He trailed one of his hands down her body, over her ribcage and down onto her belly. His fingers touched lightly, but to Elinor it felt as if they burned everywhere they touched. Then the fingers strayed lower, into the bush of curls between Elinor's legs. A place no one had touched her before; a secret, magical place. Then lower still; and Elinor's back arched involuntarily as Lucius touched a small nub of flesh beneath her curls. The feeling was intense, too intense to allow her to lie quietly, but at the same time it was incredible.

'There,' she said breathlessly. 'Touch there again.'

Instead of touching it with the tip of a finger, as he had done the time before, Lucius slid his whole hand between her thighs, so that his palm rested firmly against that remarkable place. He moved his hand in tiny circles and the feeling, though less consuming, was building up inside her until Elinor thought she might expire from the flames inside her. And then his fingers dipped inside her, and she gasped, shivers and ecstasy taking her over as she rode on waves of fire to some distant, wonderful, horizon.

'More,' she whispered, her voice husky.

Lucius looked down on her, and stroked a tendril of hair away from her face with surprising tenderness. 'This next will hurt, just a little,' he said warningly.

'I don't care.'

He laughed. 'No, my little vixen?'

He pushed inside her with a slow motion. Elinor gave a

little gasp as she felt, quite intensely, something tear inside her. But the pain that Lucius had warned her of was less overwhelming than the pleasure which followed in its wake as he began to move. It was both too much and not enough, at the same time; Elinor wasn't sure whether she wanted to beg him for more or to plead with him to stop, now, before she lost herself forever in a place she hadn't known existed until now. It was beautiful – incredible – frightening: she felt the wet trickle of tears on her face.

'Elinor?' Lucius's voice had taken on a deeper timbre; his blond hair was dampened with sweat. She had never seen him sweat before, Elinor thought inconsequentially. It made him seem more vulnerable, somehow.

'Yes,' she murmured. 'Yes.'

'Yes,' he agreed; and his movements became faster.

Elinor's hands went up to grasp him, her fingers digging convulsively into his shoulders as he thrust inside her. She could hear the harsh sound of his breathing; her own breaths were quick and shallow and needy. Then, suddenly, Lucius gave a groan; she felt him spasm inside her, felt a warm wetness between her legs. For a moment it was as if the world stopped; then, he was rolling away, lying next to her, and she found herself staring at him as if she had never seen him before. He smiled at her.

'I'm sorry, my dear. It will be better for you next time.'

'It gets better?' Elinor felt foolish the moment the words were out of her mouth.

'Yes, very much so, I promise.'

'I don't ...' To her own bewilderment, Elinor found that she was crying; she could not have explained the reason for her tears even to herself.

She fell asleep with the tears still wet upon her face, with her mind full of nothing but the wonders of intimacy. She fell asleep thinking that her marriage might be the most wonderful thing ever to have happened to her.

Chapter Three

LUCIUS HAD LEFT THE room by the time Elinor woke up the following morning. The sun was creeping in through the crack between the curtains, lighting a path across the floor. Elinor felt warm and lazy, stretching like a contented cat as she wriggled herself up to a sitting position. She immediately became conscious of her nakedness, and leaned over the side of the bed to pick up her shift. For a second she thought ruefully of the new nightgown she had bought especially for her wedding night but had never worn; but the ruefulness was overlaid with an outrageous sense of contentment as she remembered what the previous night had brought.

When the maid had brought in hot water, and she had washed and dressed, she joined her husband at the breakfast table. Lucius appeared to be buried in a newspaper, though he put it down long enough to pour Elinor a drink.

'Thank you.' Elinor took a sip of the chocolate, and asked, 'Do we have any plans for today?'

'Do you want to relax after the exigencies of yesterday?'

'I'll admit that I wouldn't mind a quiet day,' Elinor acknowledged. 'What about you?'

'I must see the lawyer to go through a few details of our marriage settlement. Would you like to visit your mother whilst I am doing so?'

'That sounds good.' "Marriage settlement". Could anything make their wedding sound less romantic and more like a business deal? But then, of course, that was precisely what it was.

'Then, you will want to sort out your clothing and such like,' Lucius said, with the vagueness only a man could bring to the important subject of clothes.

'Certainly. Where should I put them?' Elinor asked. 'Do you already take up the closet space in the bedroom?'

'My clothes are in the next room. Indeed, I thought that you could have the bedroom we occupied last night and I could have the adjoining one, during our stays here,' Lucius said casually. 'There should be plenty of room for your clothes in the room – tell me if there isn't, and I will make arrangements.'

Elinor frowned. 'But I thought ...' She trailed off. She had thought they would share a bed, a bedroom. But when she considered the matter more fully, she remembered that Lucius's parents had always had a room apiece. It was, indeed, standard practice in upper class households: her mother and father had been unusual in that they preferred to share.

'Yes?' Lucius pressed.

'Nothing.' Elinor forced a smile. Perhaps he would join her enough that the solitary room would not seem so solitary, after all. 'I will sort my clothes out later. For the moment, go back to your paper.'

He didn't join her that night. Nor the next, nor the next. Elinor tried not to wonder whether Lucius, even in their home village, was getting his satisfaction elsewhere, with more experienced ladies. After all, despite the words in the wedding vows, Lucius had never truthfully promised fidelity. He had made that clear when he had offered for her; and Elinor could not clam that Lucius was not fulfilling his side of the agreement. Her mother could still not be considered well, but compared to her previous state of health Mrs Everton was a different woman. Rid of the constant anxiety about money, as well as being under the care of the best doctor in the county, she was gaining fitness with every day which passed.

No, Lucius had certainly kept his promise. And Elinor must keep hers: be the complaisant wife Lucius required. If she was fool enough to hope that he might ... might what? Be kept satisfied by Elinor alone, an ignorant young woman whose only sexual experience had been her wedding night? Might not care to stray, at least so soon? Even, fall in love with her? Well, if Elinor had ever hoped for any of those, let alone the last, she was a fool indeed and she deserved her disappointment.

'Idiot,' she whispered into her pillow, and determined to think no more on the subject.

It was the following week when something occurred to Elinor. If Lucius was not prepared to pleasure her ... she could at least satisfy herself to a certain degree. Some of the things he had done – the places he had touched – were surely possible for her to copy. The night could become, once more, a time of learning and sexual exploration.

The first night, she began slowly, removing her nightgown and revelling in the sensation of the soft sheets against her skin. *He had touched her lips with his ...* Her finger drifted across her lips; she sucked it into her mouth, sliding it in and out. *He ran his fingers over her breasts ...* Elinor's free hand moved up to cup her left breast, and she moved her palm all around it, conscious of the change to hardness of her nipple as her hand brushed over it again and again. She took the damp finger from her mouth and pressed it to her right nipple, her back arching a little at the sensation. It was not Lucius, it was not as good as if he were there – but there was still something stirring inside her; a tiny flicker of pleasure which Elinor intended to fan. *His hands grew firmer.* She rubbed her hand harder across her breast, squeezing it gently. The same tingles she had noticed when Lucius held her like this swept across her. Not as big, nothing like as incredible, but still ... Making her heart beat that little bit faster. Making her breathing catch, just for half a second.

'Lucius,' she whispered, remembering how he'd smelt: musky and manly. She took in a deep breath, imagining she could smell his scent on the air. 'Lucius,' she sighed again, sliding her hand down over the pale skin of her belly until it rested on the nest of auburn curls between her legs.

There was a dampness between her thighs, and she ran a finger through it, then brought it to her mouth to taste herself. Then, daringly, she pushed her fingers inside her, just a little distance, and felt how her flesh gave way to her touch. It felt ... nice. For a moment, Elinor was disappointed by "nice" – an insipid word for an insipid feeling. When Lucius had done it, it had been so much more than merely nice. Never mind. She was learning her way; Lucius knew exactly what he was doing. She wiggled her fingers experimentally, fascinated by feeling a part of her own body that she'd never touched before. There was a tingly place just above her fingers, and she pressed the palm of her hand against it. Involuntarily, her hips bucked upwards at the touch, and she caught her breath. That was unexpected. She was not entirely sure whether it was wonderful or terrible; certainly it had brought a definite response from her body. How had she never known about this? How had she never thought to try this before? She thought back to the "old" Elinor of two weeks previously. Had marriage already changed her so much? She suspected it had; and she would not change back for the world.

Soon, however, the honeymoon was over. Elinor visited her mother one last time before she and Lucius set off for London. Mrs Everton was pleased to see her, as always, and they chatted about everything under the sun – except Elinor's marriage. Elinor's mother had come to believe thoroughly that Elinor had married for love and love alone (just as Mrs Everton herself had done, so many years previously), and there was no chance that Elinor would disillusion her mother of that comfortable and comforting belief. Nevertheless, as Elinor made to leave, Mrs Everton stopped her, a pale hand on Elinor's wrist.

'I shall miss you, my darling,' she said simply.

Elinor bit her lip. For so long she and her mother had been all-in-all to each other. Even if Elinor's marriage had indeed been all her mother imagined it, Elinor would have found it hard to be parted by so many miles from her mother. As it was, Elinor had a sick sense of dread about the prospective move to London for the Season. It was so long since her solitary début year there, and her life had changed beyond imagining during those missing years. She felt disconnected, uncertain whether the "society manners" which had once been so natural to her would return at will.

'I will miss you too,' she said finally, smiling down at the still wan face of her mother. 'But I can go with my mind at ease to see you looking so much healthier.'

Mrs Everton tapped the back of Elinor's hand admonishingly. 'I will manage quite nicely without you. You are not to spend your precious time with Lucius worrying about your silly old mother.'

'No, mamma,' Elinor said obediently, her eyes sparkling with mischief. 'But I suppose I am allowed occasionally to think of my "silly old mother", especially since I am peculiarly fond of her? And maybe even – since I am being daring – to address a letter to her, now and then?'

Her mother laughed. 'I think that might possibly be acceptable, you awful child.'

Elinor leaned down and kissed her mother's forehead affectionately. 'You will look after yourself, and I shall look after myself, and we will neither of us worry about the other.'

'I have no intention of worrying about you,' Mrs Everton said serenely. 'I will be imagining you having the time of your life with Lucius – just as you deserve.'

Elinor said her farewells and left, determined that she would not cry. In which determination she was *almost* successful.

To her surprise, Elinor enjoyed London. There was no reason, of course, why she should not have done so – but it had not crossed her mind that she should. Taken up with the thoughts of her mother's delicate health and her own unexpected marriage, not to mention the massive changes which had happened to her entire life in the last few months, her predominant feeling had been a determination to make everything work for all the parties involved. Her own enjoyment had not been on the agenda.

Lucius did not visit her room in London any more than he had done, after that first night, in the country, but Elinor was resigned to that now. If he had not needed to gain satisfaction in her arms in the country, he would hardly wish to do so in London where his alternative options were that much broader. Meanwhile, she continued her solitary explorations of her own body, and told herself that it was enough. Although Lucius did not want her, she had no intention of attempting to find solace with another man. Aside from the fact that she owed him that much in return for all he had done for her, there never had been any other man for Elinor, whether she liked to admit it or not. It was his name she whispered when a certain touch of her fingers sent shivers through her body; his mouth that she imagined on her own; his hands ...

She had had one night of pleasure. More than she had ever hoped for or expected. She would be content with that.

Elinor was interested, though not altogether shocked, to discover that Lucius himself was not universally popular. Sometimes she wasn't certain that *she* altogether liked him; she was in love with him, certainly, but he regularly annoyed and frustrated her. The ladies of the *ton* appeared to fall into three separate groups: those who enjoyed his company, and his reputation as a roué, without ever having been attracted to him; those who had once liked him more, perhaps, than they should, and who now regretted it; and those who looked upon Elinor as an interloper, and the only reason why Lucius would not now be marrying them. The middle category was unnervingly large: Elinor wondered sometimes whether Lucius could really have flirted with – seduced? – quite so many ladies. Their attitudes towards her ranged from pitying, through resentful, to out-and-out catty. If Elinor had not known the nature of the gentleman she had married, she thought often, she would soon have been made aware.

'Mr Crozier's new little wife.' Belinda Dolinger had been one of the first "ladies" to use her conversation with Elinor to express her contempt of Elinor's husband.

Irritating though she had found this expression, Elinor was uncertain, so early on, of Miss Dolinger's intentions. She had, therefore, bitten her tongue and refrained from suggesting that not only was she not little, but that she was also Mr Crozier's *only* wife.

'That is correct,' she'd said, nodding politely to her new acquaintance.

'We all pity you, you know,' Belinda had continued with a tinkling laugh.

'Really?'

'Oh, marry in haste, repent at leisure, you understand,' Belinda explained. 'Your marriage was very sudden, Mrs Crozier, was it not?'

Elinor gave her a self-possessed smile – a talent which would become an art form over more conversations with the poisonous Belinda. 'Hardly. We've been acquainted since childhood.'

'Oh Heavens, you mean he married a country girl from that backwater village of his?' Miss Dolinger clasped her hands to her mouth as if the words had accidentally been forced from her, rather than being – as Elinor suspected –

utterly intentional.

'That is one way of putting it,' said Lucius dryly, coming up behind Miss Dolinger in time to hear the last line. He put an arm around Elinor's waist. 'Though you might remember Mrs Crozier from her Season in London three years ago, when she was Miss Everton.' He smiled. 'Except of course she attended the best parties, Belinda; something that you have never done. Good evening.'

He gently manoeuvred Elinor away, much to her indignation.

'If she didn't hate me before that, she's certain to now,' Elinor commented crossly. 'Really, Lucius, that was unacceptably rude.'

'And what was she?' asked Lucius. 'I merely shared a little of the truth with her, Elinor.'

Yes, thought Elinor, a very little. For although it was true that she was as well born as any of the ladies present, it was equally true that directly before her marriage her circumstances had been nowhere near as salubrious.

'And besides,' Lucius added calmly, 'she would never have liked you anyway. I suspect the only person Belinda Dolinger truly loves is herself.'

Belinda's overt unpleasantness, however, was more easily dealt with than the subtle digs Elinor received from other women. She put the majority of them down to jealousy: she saw how almost every unattached lady – and many an attached one – kept their eyes on Lucius as he did the rounds at balls and card evenings. She could not blame them, really: she was no less easily attracted by the wretched gentleman she had married. And they weren't to know, she thought resignedly, that he'd married her in *order* to keep his options open, rather than to cut off his other female options. Lucius's popularity with the gentlemen, too, was mixed. He had a wide range of friends, many of them ladies' men themselves, such as Lord Argett and Mr Black; but Elinor was also intrigued to meet other gentlemen, ones whom she saw outside the usual social occasions.

One such was Octavius Wootten. Elinor thought on first meeting him that she did not like the gentleman. He was sullen-faced, reserved and unfriendly. Then he smiled at something she said, and his whole face changed. She learned later that he was severely shy and all too aware of his own defects, whilst not appreciating his attributes as much as he should. In many ways, he seemed an unusual friend for outgoing, confident Lucius; but neither man seemed aware of the incongruity and it was certainly no one-sided friendship on Wootten's part. If anything, Lucius deferred more to Wootten than the other way around, and Elinor was fascinated by this new insight into her husband. As well as having the light charm which made him so popular, Lucius demonstrated in his dealings with Wootten that he was also well-read, thoughtful and with a generosity of spirit that few people would associate with him. The pair of them donated large sums of money to one of the London workhouses. Wootten was on the board of the committee; Lucius kept his involvement considerably more secret but, Elinor suspected, provided more in the way of cash than he acknowledged.

And yet, just as Lucius turned out to have hidden depths of seriousness that Elinor had not expected, she found Wootten better and better company as she began to know him more. He was not, it seemed, quite so solemn and worthy as she first imagined; instead having a wry sense of humour, and a sarcastic wit which made many things he said worth considering twice: the obvious meaning might not be the only way in which one could take his words.

But not all gentlemen appreciated Lucius. At a ball one evening, Elinor spent a good deal of her time fascinated by the byplay between her husband and a gentleman whose name, it seemed, was Sir Hugo Mansfield. Lucius had bowed coldly to him at the beginning of the evening, and been given a colder bow still in return. When the pair met at the card table, the stakes seemed to be considerably higher in emotional value than in currency, though both, it seemed, were known gamblers who regularly played for large sums. Yet the atmosphere between them was tangible, deep dislike pouring off them both in a way that Elinor could see no reason for. Sir Hugo seemed in every other way completely unexceptionable: he was tall and handsome, with good dress sense, and a pleasant smile. Lucius rose from the table a winner; and it seemed only the obligation of good manners was enough to make Sir Hugo shake his hand at the end of the game.

'Sir Hugo Mansfield seems to dislike you intensely,' Elinor commented in the carriage on the way home.

'Yes.' Lucius leaned back against the sumptuous seat. 'He resents me because he believes I stole his mistress.'

'Oh,' Elinor said blankly, wondering whether all husbands were as open about their peccadillos as Lucius. Though, she thought ruefully, she was not precisely the usual sort of wife. Lucius had made it clear when marrying her that he intended to continue womanising: she had been bought and paid for to find it acceptable. 'Did you?' she asked, controlling her voice in a way she felt was impressive in the circumstances.

'In a way,' he said. Elinor wondered how there could possibly be a middle ground in such things. Surely one either had a mistress or did not? Lucius was clearly aware of her thoughts, and smiled at her before continuing. 'I assisted her to get out of a situation not to her liking.' He paused, clearly wondering how much more to say. 'He hurt her,' he said coolly. 'Sometimes with whips or knives.'

'Oh,' said Elinor again; then, in an attempt to live up to Lucius's savoir faire, she added, 'I take it she did not wish him to?'

'No.' There was a flash of anger in Lucius's eyes, and he spat the word sharply. 'No,' he said again, this time more calmly, 'she did *not* wish him to.' Elinor said no more, slightly ashamed of her question; and after a minute or two had passed, Lucius spoke again, in the polite tones of a stranger. 'I trust you had a pleasant evening?'

'Yes,' she said, wishing she hadn't gone at all; wishing she'd never married this gentleman with his moods and his complicated history. 'Yes, a very pleasant evening.'

It was three nights later when Elinor, waiting for her most recent dance partner to fetch her a glass of champagne, overheard a conversation between Miss Dolinger and a couple of her friends.

'I never did think much of Crozier,' Miss Dolinger announced, 'but surely he could have done better than that squat little wife of his. After all of those inamoratas, well known for their beauty, as well! I don't know how he could.'

'Well, Jane Fevell says that Miss Shaw's sister saw Crozier with that actress last week,' one of the other ladies commented. 'You know, the one who's making so many of the gentlemen's heads turn.'

'And it's not for the quality of her *acting*,' squealed Miss Dolinger happily. 'Well, that doesn't surprise me. It wouldn't take Crozier long to set up a new mistress, given what he has to go home to.'

Elinor's partner returned with the drink, and Elinor gratefully moved out of earshot of Belinda Dolinger. Of course, it was perfectly reasonable that Lucius should be bedding another woman: he had certainly made it clear that fidelity was not on the agenda. But still, it hurt. It hurt more, too, to have it society gossip – surely, thought Elinor grumpily, the least Lucius might have managed was to keep his affairs private. It only occurred to her considerably later that Miss Dolinger and her satellites might have known that she was close enough to overhear them; but that consoled her very little. She nevertheless had no reason to doubt the information

It was more comforting when Elinor was granted tickets

for Almacks – that holy of holies for everyone who wanted to count as *someone*. Why the exclusivity of Almacks made up for the fact that the balls were very tepid affairs, and the refreshments extremely uninteresting, no one could quite say. The fact was, however, that being given tickets to the place assured one of claiming a high place in society. Elinor had a shrewd suspicion that her disagreements with Belinda Dolinger had assisted her to gain such a prize: the Princess Esterházy, one of the guardians of Almacks, had a barely disguised loathing for Miss Dolinger, whom she saw as distinctly common in her manners and ways, even if not by birth. Elinor suspected strongly that she was invited to Almacks more as a slap in the face for the vulgar Belinda than because of her own merits. It didn't hurt, either, of course, that several of the middle-aged ladies who ran the place had an undeniable fondness for Lucius; but Elinor preferred not to think about that. Too many people were fond of Lucius, and Elinor would not be jealous, she would *not*.

On nights when they did not go out together, Lucius often went out on his own. True to her promises, Elinor resisted the desperate urge to demand where he was going – and with whom – but it hurt a little bit more each time he went. He was polite enough, invariably inquiring whether she would be all right without him, but Elinor thought he seemed more distant on these evenings. She wondered, painfully, whether he was distancing himself from her before cheating on her: a sort of mental retreat. But then, why would he need to? Maybe he just hated being in her company. There had been evenings before when she knew perfectly well that Lucius had had no intention of going out; yet after an hour or so with her, he abruptly got up. One in particular stood out.

'I'm going out for a bit,' he had said abruptly.

Elinor was shocked. They had been in the middle of a

conversation about the latest ladies fashion – perhaps not the most thrilling topic for a gentleman, although he seemed to know a great deal about the subject – but still, surely not so terribly dull that he felt obliged to leave the house to escape from her? He could, after all, just have changed the subject.

'That's sudden,' she'd said weakly.

He appeared to be glaring at her; Elinor could not for the life of her understand what she had done to make him so angry.

'I need some fresh air.' He had left at once, not even thinking to take a cape with him, though the night was cold.

After that, Elinor had noticed that whenever they had no plans for an evening, Lucius usually found some excuse to go out alone. Hurt, but determined not to show it, she made it clear that it was irrelevant to her whether he was present or not.

'I'll be fine,' she reassured him that evening through gritted teeth. 'A quiet evening in with a book is just what I need.'

When he had gone, she looked down at her book – Maria Edgeworth's *A Vindication Of The Rights Of Women* – and wondered where it had all gone wrong. Frustrated at her own mood, she decided to put aside the book and write to her mother.

Dear Mamma ...

Elinor looked at the first line and wondered what she could say. So much had happened in London, but the nuances were such that she wasn't sure what to mention. She was used to confiding almost everything in her mother, but her marriage had been the first break in this, and now – now Elinor was looking at a white sheet of paper and wondered how she could fill it.

It was lovely to get your note today. It sounds like you are

*doing really well – I'm so glad, dear. I laughed at your
description of the neighbours falling over each other to
visit; your pen can be very cruel! Remind me not to get on
your bad side.*

All is well here, too. Lucius is –

Elinor stopped again. "Nice to me", she had been going to
write; but since in her mother's eyes this was a love match,
Mrs Everton would expect nothing less. Indeed, even to
mention it might set alarm bells ringing for her mother, who
was no fool. Elinor would do anything to keep from
worrying her. Better Mrs Everton might be; well, she
certainly was not. After careful thought, Elinor continued:

– in his element in London society.

Then, smiling, for her mother had told her that she read the
Society pages of the papers, she added:

*If you are wondering how much of the gossip in the
newspapers is true, approximately half. But as Lucius loves
people to be uncertain as to which half, I will leave that
decision with you. There is much, however, that the news
does not say*

And Elinor told a little about the interest Lucius took in the
poorer parts of the city, realising to her shame how little she
herself knew.

Then, turning to lighter matters, she told her mother
about the modistes she had visited and the astronomical
number of new dresses she now owned.

*– And hats, Mamma! Truly, I have a hat for every occasion.
I tell Lucius I shall never need to buy another, but he laughs
and returns with further new offerings to tempt me with.*

105

Mamma would like that: although she knew that Lucius was rich enough to buy a dozen hats each day and not notice the expense, Mrs Everton – like Elinor herself, if truth be told – would appreciate the gesture.

By the time the letter was finished, Elinor had written herself, as well as (she hoped) her mother, into a feeling of fondness for Lucius; and smiling ruefully, decided that however much of Maria Edgeworth's polemic she might sympathise with, nonetheless life as a rich lady was not so hard.

She returned to her reading with less enthusiasm, and was easily disturbed by the sound of a footman opening a door. It was too early for Lucius to return, but surely too late for any casual visitor? Had anything happened? Anything bad? When Wootten was announced, she stood to greet him with some anxiety.

'Has something happened to Lucius?' she demanded.

'I beg your pardon?' Wootten looked confused for a second. 'Oh. No, nothing like that. I apologise if my late arrival concerned you. I wanted to have a few words with Lucius about the governors' meeting at the workhouse in a fortnight's time. I gather he is not at home, however?'

'No.' Elinor bit her lip to prevent herself saying more. Evidently one of the people that Lucius was not out with was Wootten. Which made it even more likely that he was with one of his inamoratas.

Wootten smiled ruefully. 'It was a faint hope, I suppose. I admit that I often forget that other people enjoy the parts of London society that I find tedious in the extreme.'

'Like women?' The words slipped out before Elinor could prevent them.

'Come now, that is unfair. You know by now – at least I presume you do –' Wootten added, 'that I very much enjoy your company.'

'That wasn't precisely what I meant,' said Elinor dryly.

A faint colour spread across Wootten's cheeks. 'Oh.' He

recovered himself. 'I acknowledge that that is not an area I have a great deal of experience in.'

'Unlike my husband.' Wootten hesitated, and Elinor felt ashamed to have put him in such an embarrassing situation. Keeping her voice light, she added, 'It is all right. You need to hide nothing from me. I know he has mistresses.'

Wootten looked at her. 'Yes,' he said, 'he had – before his marriage.'

Elinor sighed. Wootten – bless the man – was an idealist. The idea that anyone might not have married for love did not occur to him. She caught herself up. Wootten was on the committee of a workhouse in one of the poorest parts of London: an idealist he might be, but he was not ignorant. Say, then, something different: it would not occur to Wootten that his dear friend, Lucius, might have married for any other reason than love.

'It is fine,' she assured him, smiling. 'I do not mind.'

Wootten went to speak, then stopped.

'What?' Elinor demanded.

'It doesn't matter,' he said.

'Tell me,' she urged.

'I was going to say,' Wootten said uncomfortably, 'that perhaps you should mind.' As Elinor's smile faded, he added, 'You will say it is none of my business, and you will, of course, be right. But I am fond of you, and it seems a pity ... Well. It is none of my business.'

Elinor looked at his flushed, embarrassed face and appreciated the honesty which had led him to speak. 'Thank you for caring,' she said gently, 'but I'm afraid my marriage is no one's business but my own.'

'And Lucius's.'

'Oh yes,' said Elinor, her tone grim. 'Certainly his.'

'Forgive me,' Wootten said. 'I should not have spoken.'

She placed a hand gently on his arm. 'I appreciate your intentions, Mr Wootten. You are an extremely decent gentleman and I'm glad to count you a friend.'

He laughed. 'If I have to be given a brush off, I prefer your way of effecting it, Mrs Crozier. I too am glad to count you a friend.'

He bowed, and left her. Strangely, Elinor thought, he had made her less distressed. Certainly he had said nothing that gave her any hope that Lucius was not having affairs, but that was not the point. He had reminded her, unintentionally, with his mention of the workhouse Lucius and he took an interest in, that there were indeed people considerably worse off than herself; and his gently offered friendship was something she treasured. Perhaps things were not quite so bad.

Two days later, driving out with Lucius in the park, Elinor had a memorable, unpleasant experience. Drawing up the horses, Lucius turned to her.

'You see the lady over to your left?' he said quietly.

Elinor looked. "Lady" was perhaps not the word she would have used for someone who was evidently a member of the oldest profession, albeit undeniably an upmarket version thereof. The woman's clothes were rich and beautiful and she wore them well, but they were considerably too revealing for modesty.

She nodded, wondering for one bleak second whether Lucius was about to reveal the identity of his latest mistress. She could not complain if he did so; but oh, she did not wish to know. The woman was pretty – would have been called beautiful if it were not for the fact that her face was marred by a scar which puckered the corner of her left eye on its way down towards her ear. Elinor wondered, for a brief moment, whether Lucius would be attracted to *her* if she wore such clothes. She was not as well proportioned, certainly – but then she did not have that scar.

'Yes,' she said.

'Sir Hugo did that.' Lucius's voice was dispassionate. 'The scar. She has others, too, thanks to his treatment of her.

She told me he got harder faster if she bled and wept. Sometimes he used her blood to coat his erection before he took her.'

Elinor felt a wave of nausea overtake her, feeling guilty for her earlier comparison of the woman's looks to her own. 'That's the woman ...' She trailed off, but Lucius understood her question.

'That is the 'mistress' I stole from him, yes. You may think, of course – as Mansfield did – that the fact that she is a courtesan means that she does not deserve anything better.'

'No,' Elinor said quietly. 'No, I do not think that.'

'I wanted you to understand,' he said simply, and turned back to the horses, urging them on once more.

Although Elinor had been silenced on the occasion of her seeing the courtesan, there was one way in which her usual relationship with Lucius had changed very little since their childhood. They had always verbally sparred. Elinor had never wished to allow Lucius to best her in a war of words; he, it was evident, felt the same way. There was an element of teasing in their battle: often one would make a comment which the other knew perfectly well was not something they believed, for the purposes of annoying their spouse or winning an argument. Elinor supposed that perhaps they should have grown past the age of bickering like children; but it was one of the ways in which Lucius always had made her feel more alive, more fired up – and that certainly had not altered, though the experience of the feelings themselves had grown and changed.

She remembered a case in their long distant past when, angered by a claim Lucius had made, she had grabbed a fencing foil from its stand and attacked. Elinor had always said afterwards that it was not that he had beaten her quite easily with his own foil – that, of course, was to be expected: he had had considerably more practice with the implement than she. But he had toyed with her for a couple of minutes, allowing her to think that she might have some chance of winning before flicking the foil from her grasp: it was that which had frustrated her about the encounter.

Tonight's argument was on the subject of literature. As they left dinner, therefore, they were arguing about the quality of John Milton's *Paradise Lost* and his *Paradise Regained*. Elinor was determined that the former was considerably the more interesting of the books.

She swept over to the table where her copy of *Paradise Lost* lay, and began to read:

> "*Receive thy new possessor: One who brings*
> *A mind not to be changed by place or time.*
> *The mind is its own place, and in itself*
> *Can make a Heaven of Hell, a Hell of Heaven.*
> *What matter where, if I be still the same?*"

'I find the idea that one can create a happy life for oneself no matter what the external circumstances uplifting. I have a great deal of time for Milton's Satan.'

'Of course you sympathise with the devil,' Lucius agreed blandly, leaning casually against the mantelpiece. 'After all, you are a woman.'

Elinor knew he was only trying to provoke her, but he was nevertheless successful in his aim. The book was still in her hand, and she walked across and without warning slapped it against him. She made contact, then heard a muffled cry, and looked over her shoulder to see Lucius doubled up in pain.

'There is no need for theatrics,' she scolded him, presuming him once again to be faking his anguish to catch her off guard, just as he had faked a clumsiness with a foil all those years ago. 'It was a gentle slap – and well deserved, I must say.'

Lucius, his hands pressed to his groin, glared at her. 'I

assure you that I am not overacting. Do you know what it feels like to …' He cut off. 'Of course, you wouldn't. As we have just been agreeing, you are a lady. However, let me inform you for your future information that there are some parts of a man where the gentlest slap can hurt – even when not assisted by the sharp corner of an unnecessarily heavy book.'

'Oh.' Elinor paused, realising where she must have caught him, and utterly mortified. She hesitated, unsure whether to flee for her bedroom or to try and undo the damage caused. But she couldn't stroke him *there*. Goodness knew she had trouble enough keeping her thoughts away from his body at the best of time, without touching him in such an intimate position. She could feel her face burning with embarrassment as she said guiltily 'I am so sorry.'

Her evident discomfiture placated her husband a little, and his frown eased.

'A lesson well learnt on both sides,' he said. 'I shall remember in future not to insult you, or any woman – at least unless I am standing a good distance away and am prepared to make my escape,' he added, his voice sardonic, but his mouth curling into the beginnings of a smile. 'And you will remember that despite a man's fabled strength compared to a lady, there are some areas in which we are weaker than water.'

Chapter Four

FOR ONCE, IT WAS Elinor's turn to be going out without Lucius. The card party she was attending had said clearly on the invitation that it was "ladies only". She had suggested to Lucius that she might refuse, but he had encouraged her to accept.

Elinor had, in her secret heart, hoped that Lucius would show some indignation – perhaps make a scene as a jealous husband and tell her that she could not possibly go out without him. Even when she had resigned herself to his disinterest, it felt peculiar to go out as a single lady. Although she had met with people during the day time alone, any evening engagements she had attended had always been with the accompaniment of Lucius. She wondered, for a dismal second, whether they were already growing further apart than they had been when they married. Four months into a marriage, and already the cracks were beginning to show. Lucius, who had told her coolly that he had an early evening meeting with a couple of gentlemen acquaintances at his club, had taken the carriage and the usual driver, but he had organised another one especially for her. Elinor knew she ought to feel grateful for his assiduousness in looking after her – at least one of the ladies of her acquaintance had a husband whose policy was that if he wished to go out alone, she would have to stay at home. Things could be worse, she reminded herself, even if it did feel as if Lucius cared little whether she went or stayed.

The footman escorted her down the steps of the house and helped her into the carriage. Before she could thank him, the driver had clicked his tongue at the horses and they were moving. But not far. Around the next corner, the driver drew up again.

'Why have you stopped?' she called. Either the driver was deaf or he was ignoring her, because she got no reply. Instead, the door of the carriage was pulled open by a scruffy looking man with greasy hair. 'Excuse me. I think you mistake yourself,' Elinor said haughtily.

'Nah, I don't,' the man replied, looking her up and down. 'Mrs Crozier, aren't you?'

'I do not think my identity is any of your business.' Elinor realised the carriage had started moving again and rapped on the window. 'Driver, stop! Please. Oh *listen*, won't you?' she cried crossly.

'He's not going to listen,' said the man beside her. 'He's being paid too well.'

'Mr Crozier arranged – this?' Elinor demanded in disbelief. When Lucius had arranged for a carriage, he surely hadn't arranged as well for a – a what? An escort? An escort who looked like a petty thief? This was a joke, and it wasn't a funny one.

'Oh yeah, sorry about that an' all. The carriage "his nibs" arranged had a bit of an accident. Terrible thing,' said the man conversationally, running a grimy hand down Elinor's arm in a manner which unnerved her more than she liked to admit. 'Quite indisposed, or whatever yeh posh word is.'

'I don't understand,' said Elinor, having a sudden bad feeling that she did.

'Yes, you do,' he said, confirming the unspoken anxiety. 'Didn't I tell you? This ain't a trip to a card party. This is a kidnap.'

Elinor's first feeling on hearing the words said aloud, despite the fact that it confirmed what she had been beginning to fear, was sheer disbelief. One simply did not get abducted in a smart carriage at seven o'clock in the evening. Surely abductions should be carried out late at night, or with someone important?

'What is happening?' she demanded imperiously. 'Who are you?'

The man smiled, giving Elinor a good look at his yellowing and rotted teeth. 'Call me Ted,' he suggested. As to the rest, you'll find out. Nice girl like you, you'll find out.' He ran his hand down her arm again, and Elinor shuddered.

'Please keep your hands to yourself.'

'Oh, it's "please" now. I like a lady with manners,' Ted replied, moving his hand across her front until it rested across her right breast. Elinor slapped it away, and he caught her arm in his grasp. 'Now, you shouldn't ha' done that, should you? That wasn't polite, was it?' He twisted her arm a little bit, and Elinor bit heavily into her lip to prevent herself from crying out in pain. 'Remember them nice manners your mam taught you.'

'Where are we going?' Elinor fought to keep her tone even, though it was pitched several tones higher than usual. 'Please,' she added again, hoping to appease the man.

He let go of her arm, but did not answer the question. Elinor turned to look out of the window: they were heading into a part of London she did not know – and which, by the look of the run-down buildings and dirty streets, she felt quite lucky not to have known before. Dusk had fallen, but there were few lights visible. At another time, Elinor might have found it spooky; at the moment, she was too bound up in what was happening to her to care much about any ghostly imaginings.

The driver pulled up outside a grubby looking house, and Ted stepped out. Elinor considered, for a moment, trying to run; but she knew that she would not get far before they caught her. It would be a pointless gesture, and she preferred to keep her options open for a more hopeful situation later.

'Get out,' ordered Ted gruffly. Elinor obeyed. He grabbed her shoulder and propelled her firmly towards the door of the house, turning to say to the driver 'Now, be off with you,' in a voice which brooked no argument.

'Why have you brought me here?' she asked softly as Ted opened the door with a rusty-looking key.

'Why …' replied a new and familiar voice from inside, 'I invited you here to meet me.'

Sir Hugo Mansfield. Elinor stilled. This was unexpected indeed. She had presumed that Ted had kidnapped her, hoping for Lucius to hand over money for her safe return. But Sir Hugo was as rich as Lucius himself; monetary gain could not be his motive. Which left – what? Elinor remembered Lucius's story of the beaten mistress; remembered the sight of the woman in question. Suddenly she found it hard to swallow past the lump in her throat. Was she to be beaten in revenge for Lucius's protection of the other woman? Scarred, even?

'This is a surprise.' Despite herself, Elinor could not keep her voice from trembling.

'Come in,' Sir Hugo invited coolly. He nodded at Ted. 'You have performed your part well. I thank you.'

It was as clear a dismissal as Ted's had been to the coachman. The man vanished through a door on one side of the corridor, and Elinor followed Sir Hugo into a room on the opposite side. The room was surprisingly clean, albeit most of the furniture was old and in need of mending. A chaise longue lay on one side of the room, startling in its difference to the rest of the room. It looked new, and had certainly cost considerably more money than the rest of the pieces put together. Its red cover gleamed in the light of the candles scattered around the room.

'Please,' Elinor said, attempting a gentleness she did not feel, 'tell me what this is about.'

'But where are my manners?' Sir Hugo said. 'Mrs Crozier, do take a seat.'

He gestured towards the chaise longue; Elinor, after a second's deliberation, sat herself in an old arm chair, which smelt faintly of mould. There was something wrong, something alarming, about the chaise. Like Sir Hugo himself, it did not fit the room, and unaccountably the sight of it made her nervous.

'Why am I here?'

'So that I may enjoy the pleasure of your company,' Sir Hugo drawled. 'Can you doubt it?'

'Yes,' said Elinor. 'Now, the truth, if you please.' She kept her tone firm but non-threatening as she continued, 'You have abducted me, and I would like to know the reason why.'

'Succinctly put. I have always admired the bluntness of your conversation, Mrs Crozier. Let me be equally explicit.' Sir Hugo was still standing; he strolled back and forth as he talked, as if giving a public lecture. 'You will be aware, of course, of the mutual dislike – I think I could go so far as to say "loathing" – between your husband and me?'

'Yes.'

'And the reason?'

'You feel that he stole your mistress.'

Sir Hugo raised an eyebrow. 'My my, he has been frank with you, has he not? Tell me, were you shocked to discover that your husband had a mistress?'

'Hardly,' Elinor retorted.

'No, I suspected as much. After all, I imagine it was a role you filled usefully in your time.' Sir Hugo paused. 'The only fascination really is why he took it into his head actually to marry you.'

For the first time since she had been kidnapped, fury trumped fear in Elinor's heart. 'How dare you?' Involuntarily she rose to her feet, her fists clenched at her side. 'I have never been Lucius's mistress. How dare you imply it?'

'I appear to have hit a raw nerve. I apologise, Mrs Crozier. It must only be since your marriage that –'

'When one is married, Sir Hugo, one does not count as a

116

mistress,' Elinor shot at him.

'Or at any rate, not with that particular man,' Sir Hugo agreed coolly.

'What do you mean?'

'I imagine he passes you around all his friends, does he not?' The clear cultured voice of Sir Hugo made the obscenity of his words almost worse, Elinor thought, sickened. 'Wootten, after all – it is evident to the poorest intelligence that he could not get a woman except by proxy. Does it thrill you, Mrs Crozier, having Wootten's clammy skin pressed to yours? Are you excited by each new man who touches you, thinking about what they will do to you; what you will do to them?'

'No.' Elinor's voice was a mere whisper.

'Your husband is a generous man, in his way. How many gentlemen have you had since your marriage?' he pressed on. 'Five? Ten? More? How many friends – *close* friends, you understand – does Crozier have?'

This wasn't happening. This could not be happening. Sir Hugo was a gentleman, even if an unpleasant one. No gentleman could stand and make such accusations towards a lady. This was a bad dream. Elinor blinked a couple of times in the hope the image would fade. It didn't.

'Don't. Please ...' She hated herself for begging. Hated him for bringing her to this point.

'Do you go down on your knees to each one in turn while the rest look on?' Then, as Elinor did not reply, 'Oh, come now, Mrs Crozier. There are only you and I present. No one will know what you tell me – unless you tell them, of course. But I do not think you will.'

'What is your intent?' Elinor's voice was low.

Sir Hugo smiled. 'To have a little of what all those other men have had, Mrs Crozier. Nothing more.'

'But I haven't ... I never ...' Elinor broke off, knowing that whatever she said Sir Hugo would not believe her. Knowing that his own life was such that he couldn't imagine

117

there was such a thing as a virtuous lady – let alone a married one. Let alone one married to Lucius.

'Mrs Crozier!' Sir Hugo's tone of disbelief confirmed all her fears.

'You will not believe me, will you? Whatever I say.'

Sir Hugo raised an eyebrow. 'It depends what you say. If you choose to tell me the truth, I might. If you persist in these tedious denials, however ...'

'I see,' Elinor said dully.

'Shall we start again?' Sir Hugo said kindly. 'Now, Mrs Crozier, why do we not cut to the chase? You married a libertine, whose ways are well known to the whole *ton*. Pray do not claim that you know nothing of it.'

His words hit Elinor like a slap. The whole of the polite world had been laughing at her ever since her marriage. Lucius's affairs were the worst kept secret in London ... the only secret was her role in his life.

'And then?'

'Well, I owe your companion on the journey here something for his assistance. I'm sure you understand that. But after that? You are free to go, of course.'

'Lucius will kill you.'

Sir Hugo's smile grew broader. 'Oh, I doubt it. I am reckoned a good shot, you know. And besides, you would have to tell him what has occurred here. If you choose to do so, it will be worth it for that moment alone – I do so wish I could be present at that conversation.'

'You are evil. A horrible, evil man.'

'And you, my dear Mrs Crozier, are being commonplace. A disappointment, I confess.'

Elinor's eyes had been darting round the room as the conversation took place, looking for any means of escape. But Sir Hugo was no fool, and there was no obvious way out, save past the man (no, he was not a gentleman, no matter his rank) himself. He made a move towards her, and she shrank back before she could stop herself.

'You need not concern yourself. I am a considerate lover,' Sir Hugo said. Elinor tried not to think of Lucius's animadversions on the man, wanted to wipe from her mind the image of the woman she had seen, scars still visible from Sir Hugo's treatment of her. 'And it is hardly as if the role is new to you, after all.' He put a hand into an inner pocket of his coat, and drew out a wicked looking blade. It shone silver in the candlelight, small and deadly. 'We can do this the easy way, or we can choose a more painful route, Mrs Crozier. The choice is yours.'

Elinor sank back down into the lumpy arm chair. For the first time, she realised just how serious Sir Hugo was. Up unto that point, she had thought that if, perhaps, she found the right combination of words, he might let her go. But the sight of the sharp steel glinting in front of her told her that this had been a vain hope. He would not let her go. He would never let her go until he had done what he chose to her. And even then ... she thought of the rotting teeth and dirty nails of the man called Ted, who was "owed" by Sir Hugo for his kidnap of her, and felt sick.

Finding it hard to swallow past a lump in her throat, she did her best to smile. 'Please, do not think I am challenging you,' she said, fighting to keep a quavering note from her voice. 'It is all so – unexpected, you understand.' She gave a laugh that sounded false even to her own ears. 'I was anticipating a card party, not a ... a flirtation.'

'That's what Crozier calls it these days, is it?' Sir Hugo said, his loathing for Lucius evident in every syllable. 'How refined of him. A "flirtation". Such a *nice* phrase.'

'I don't know what you mean,' Elinor said instinctively.

'Yes.' Sir Hugo's voice was suddenly low and intense. 'Yes you do, Mrs Crozier. Why do you persist in these denials? Do you think to protect that man – that so-called-man to whom you are married?'

'I apologise.' Elinor's voice wobbled a little. *Forgive me, Lucius, for what I am about to say.* 'I am accustomed, you understand, to defending my husband. It feels most strange to be in a position where I need not do any such thing.'

Sir Hugo leaned against the wall. 'Believe me, there is certainly no need to do so in my presence.' His voice became gentler, though his fingers still stroked the flat edge of the knife. 'Come, this is surely no terrifying ordeal; certainly it need not be. You never know, you might even enjoy yourself.'

'Perhaps.' Elinor wished she knew how to look coy; she looked up at Sir Hugo from under lidded eyes and hoped her expression was seductive enough. 'Why do you not show me what you know? If you are as talented as you sound, I may very well take pleasure in it. I must confess that I have not enjoyed many sexual experiences with gentlemen before now.' Which last was true enough: Elinor had not had the chance to experience more than one. If Sir Hugo chose to take her words with a different meaning, why, that was his prerogative. Lucius's words came back to her: *there is one area in which we are weaker than water.* So help me, Lucius, she thought desperately; I hope you are right.

'You are very easily persuaded,' Sir Hugo said, a note of suspicion in his voice.

Elinor gave an insouciant shrug. 'As you say, you are hardly suggesting something I am not accustomed to.' She allowed her eyes to look him up and down. 'And, indeed, you are certainly considerably more handsome than the majority of my conquests.' She allowed a note of admiration to creep into her voice. A stroke of brilliance occurred to her: one which she thought might convince Sir Hugo more than anything else she had said so far. 'And maybe,' she murmured, coming closer to Sir Hugo and putting a hand on his arm, 'if I please you well enough, you might consider finding a – a *different* reward for my original captor.'

He laughed, and Elinor thought with relief that her tactic had worked. He believed her willing to do anything with him in the hope that she would not then have to endure the grubby hands of "Ted".

'I might consider it,' he acknowledged, a loathsome smile flickering at the corner of his lips. 'If you are a very, very good girl.' To Elinor's relief, he reached up and placed the knife on the mantelpiece. Knowing she was watching, he smiled more broadly. 'Don't think about trying to reach it,' he said coolly.

'I won't.' Elinor looked up at the blade with an expression of anxiety which was by no means faked. If her plan for escape did not succeed, she had no doubt that the knife would be used on her. 'Can't we move a little further away from it?' she pleaded, her fingers clinging to his arm as she edged away from the fireplace.

'A nervous little thing, aren't you?' Sir Hugo said, but his voice was amused rather than angry.

He moved towards the chaise longue, but instead of sweeping her onto it, as Elinor had feared he would do, he pulled her into his arms as they stood. Her heart was beating fast within her breast, and there was a slight tremble in her fingers which she could not prevent.

'I am but a woman,' she said diffidently. 'I do not like weaponry, you understand.' Then, loathing herself even for saying it, 'I am made for love-making, not violence.' She swallowed the bile that rose in her throat as she said the words aloud. Whether she escaped with her chastity unsullied or not, she knew these moments would live in her mind, humiliatingly, for too long.

'Quite so,' said Sir Hugo.

He kissed her, and Elinor closed her eyes and thought a desperate apology to Lucius, that she should submit – indeed, to seem to like – these kisses from his enemy. Her breathing was ragged, not from passion, as Sir Hugo appeared to believe, but from fear. She knew what he intended to come next; she knew what she intended to come next. They were not the same. Nevertheless, she would need to make her move soon. Sir Hugo had started to unbutton

121

her dress. She had given in to his kisses, and he seemed to believe that she welcomed them. Much longer, and the opportunity might be lost.

'My Lord ...' Elinor's voice sounded weak and unconvincing to herself, but apparently not to Sir Hugo. He looked up at her, his face pink with arousal, and looking in Elinor's eyes like an over-dressed pig. She wondered how she could ever have thought him handsome. She swallowed hard. 'I ...'

Without warning, she brought her knee up, sharply, against his groin, hearing her petticoats rip under the strain. If she had got this wrong, his punishment would be vicious indeed. But no. She had hit the spot. Sir Hugo doubled up as the pain gathered him in, and his grasp on Elinor's dress loosened. She tugged herself away, leaving a scrap of the delicate silk still in his hand, and ran. Her original captor, to her relief, was not in sight as she dashed for the door. Sir Hugo had chosen his hidey-hole well. Elinor found herself in a part of London she knew not at all, but which was certainly one of the less salubrious places in which she had found herself. She knew she must look a sight: her dress ripped at the shoulder and dirty at the ankle, her hair trailing loose over her shoulders. If it weren't for the quality of the materials she was wearing, she thought wearily, no one would believe her to be part of the *ton*. Even as it was, she suspected that people would presume the clothes stolen.

She took another look round, and realised she hoped they would think the clothes a robbery. Wherever-she-was was not a safe place for elegantly dressed ladies of the polite world. A sick feeling arose in her throat as she wondered whether she had escaped one horror only to be plunged into another. The two men on the far side of the road were staring at her – as she watched, one nudged his companion and said something that drew a ribald laugh.

Trying to ape a confidence she did not feel, Elinor slowed her pace to a purposeful walk, as if she knew precisely where she was headed and had no doubt of her ability to get there. She was relieved to see the men turn away.

Five minutes later, she was alone. And totally, utterly, lost. All the famous landmarks of London were invisible in this world of tumble-down warehouses and broken bricks. It was like a different world; and Elinor knew that whatever happened, she would be irrevocably changed by this long, frightening walk. She had thought she knew what poverty was when she and her mother had been struggling to survive in Carryleigh, but the grimness of what surrounded her now showed her that she had barely scratched the surface. Occasionally she caught sight of a few ragged children, playing games along the alleyways, the strong Cockney accent strange to her ears. A woman came right up to her, pawing at her clothes. Her breath smelt rankly of alcohol, and Elinor pulled away hastily.

'It's all right, my lovely,' the woman croaked. 'I only want to help you.'

'I'm fine, thank you,' Elinor said, disentangling herself as hastily as she could, and feeling a wave of guilt about her mistrust of the woman's motives. Most likely the woman really did want to help – but what if she did not? 'Thank you,' she called again, louder, as she walked swiftly away.

'Come back, lovely.' The words drifted out to Elinor on the air, but she did not turn.

She walked further and further, pretending that the dampness of her eyes was due to the smoky surroundings and not to her own fear and tiredness. Darkness was coming, and Elinor had never been more afraid.

'Mrs Crozier!'

Elinor froze to hear her name spoken in the refined accents of a gentleman. For a couple of heartbeats she feared that Sir Hugo Mansfield had discovered her; for a couple more, she wondered whether that might not be preferable to what she could face otherwise.

'Elinor?' the voice said, gentle and shocked.

It was a familiar tone, certainly, but it was not Sir Hugo. Elinor looked up to see Octavius Wootten, and almost flung herself into his arms.

'Mr Wootten!' She rubbed a grimy hand across her face. 'Please,' she begged, 'take me home.'

Elinor knew few gentlemen who would manage what Wootten did. He asked no questions of her, but led her out of the back streets until they found a Hansom. It was evident that the cab driver was not inclined to be so reserved, but a look in Wootten's eye made him think twice about saying the words on the tip of his tongue. Instead, he drove them in silence to the Crozier residence, and Wootten and Elinor were equally quiet. When the driver pulled up, Wootten helped Elinor down and paid him.

'I'll see you in,' he said; the first words he had spoken to her since they got into the cab.

'Thank you.' Elinor wondered what he must think of her.

The footman opened the door, and recoiled as he saw his mistress, torn and bedraggled, with Octavius Wootten beside her.

'Is your master in?' Wootten asked calmly, as if he often experienced such situations.

'Yessir,' mumbled the footman, all in one word.

'Perhaps you would be good enough to fetch him?' The footman almost fell over himself in his hurry to get away. Wootten looked down at Elinor, and Elinor wondered again what he must be thinking.

'Why were you there?' she asked, realising all at once that she had never asked him. It had seemed like a miracle too incredible to be questioned.

'It is near the workhouse. There was a governor's meeting.' Wootten's expression was gentle. 'I won't ask the same of you, but I'll ask you one thing.'

'I owe you that,' she said, unable to meet his gaze.

'Talk to Lucius,' he said quietly.

'Yes.' Elinor's lower lip trembled, and she feared for a second that she might disgrace herself further by crying.

Wootten's hand grasped her arm for a second. 'Trust him,' he murmured, as Lucius came down the stairs. 'He trusts you.'

'Elinor!' The tone of Lucius's voice was one Elinor had never heard from him before. His usual swaggering walk broke down as he ran towards his wife.

'Lucius. Oh, Lucius.' Wootten was forgotten as Elinor found herself swept up into Lucius's arms. 'I look a mess,' she murmured, burying her head on his shoulder.

'Yes.' Lucius held her even more tightly. 'Elinor, love, what happened?'

'I ...' Elinor lifted her head and caught sight of the footman, standing open-mouthed and staring. Wootten had disappeared, and Elinor thought that she would have to show her gratitude to him another time. She was not sure what might have happened if he had not been there. 'Let's go upstairs,' she urged.

Lucius lifted her up and carried her to her room, setting her down on the bed as gently as if she were made of glass. Elinor tried to smile.

'I'm fine, really.'

'No you're not.'

'No, I'm not,' she confessed.

'I've been so worried. Elinor – tell me. Tell me everything.'

Elinor took a deep, shaky, breath and began to relate the events of the evening. Lucius grew paler as she spoke; and she found it hard to meet his eyes as she told how she had kissed Sir Hugo in an attempt to bring him close enough for her to effect her escape. His hands gripped hers ever tighter. Then, back-tracking a bit from her escape, her face averted from Lucius, Elinor told of the things Sir Hugo had said – the horrible, suggestive comments he had made over and over again.

'I will kill him,' Lucius said grimly.

Elinor gave what was supposed to be a laugh, but which came out more like a sob. 'Well, it certainly wasn't true, but I couldn't tell him that I'm so terrible that not even my own husband wants me, let alone any of his friends.'

'What did you say?' Lucius loosened his grip on her a little, allowing him to look into her face.

She smiled weakly, the expression betrayed by the tears that would insist on trickling down her cheeks. 'I'm sorry, Lucius. A decent wife wouldn't even speak of such things. But I've never been good at "decent" and it seems I'm not better at "indecent".'

'I never said that.'

Elinor shut her eyes, trying to avoid the hurt expression she could see on Lucius's face. 'You didn't need to.' She took a breath. 'Lucius, couldn't we try again?'

'I hurt you. I made you cry.' Lucius's voice was low. 'I couldn't forgive myself for that. I never thought–'

'I don't understand.' Elinor's mind was whirling. 'You hated it. Hated me. I was terrible.'

'How could you think that? It was the best night of my life. But you–'

'I was so happy,' she whispered. 'So happy. That one night. And then you turned back to other women. I didn't blame you: after all, it was our agreement. I was a wife to suit your convenience, one who would not complain about your affairs. I just hoped that sometimes there might be room for me also.'

He pulled back a little to look her straight in the eyes. 'Since the day I married you, I have never been near another woman, dearest.'

Elinor wondered whether she had fallen into a dream world, where everything she had ever wanted was given to her. 'Truthfully?'

'On my honour.' He gave a rueful smile. 'I don't say that it hasn't been extremely frustrating at times, but once I had you, could you possibly think I would need or want anyone else?'

'Yes,' she whispered, honestly.

'Octavius told me you thought so, once. I did not believe him, truth be told, but when he urged me to tell you of my love, I could not do so. Forgive me my pride, but I thought that even if you did not want me, I could gain some self-respect back by persuading you that others still did. It did nothing but hurt us both, I see now.'

'Of your ...' Elinor hesitated, wondering whether she had imagined the word. 'Love?' she repeated shakily.

'Yes. I married you because I loved you,' Lucius said, sounding almost angry. 'What other reason would I have?'

'But you said ...'

He stood up abruptly. 'What was I supposed to do? You made it clear many years ago that you disliked me. I told myself I didn't mind, made love to woman after woman in the hope it would help me get over you. But I never did. If I'd told you I loved you, would you have married me then? I knew you'd laugh in my face. But for your mother ...' He turned away. 'I knew you'd do anything for her. God help me, I took advantage, and I should not have done that. I regret it. You should have married for love, as you deserved.' He knelt beside the bed at her feet. 'Forgive me, Elinor, if you can.'

'Lucius ...' Elinor felt like she was seeing her husband for the first time. Always so cool, so collected; to see him broken and kneeling at her feet was shocking. She tumbled off the bed to fling herself down beside him. 'Don't you – did you not know? Know I was in love with you, just as I always have been. I tried to hide it, but I knew you were not convinced. Every time I came near you, you shied away.'

'I didn't trust myself.' Lucius's voice was full of shame. 'I dared not get close to you in case I could not resist the temptation of your body. God, so many nights I went out so that I would not break down and beg you to hold me.'

'My love,' she whispered, the words trembling as she spoke them for the first time. 'My love.'

'And then tonight. You would never have found yourself in the position you did today were it not for what I've done,' Lucius said, lost in his own memories and guilt. 'Can you forgive me for that, Elinor? I swear that I will do anything to win your forgiveness.'

My dear, there is nothing to forgive. I ...' Her voice trembled as she remembered the afternoon's experiences. 'I am glad you assisted another woman to get away from Sir Hugo. I cannot bear the thought of anyone being forced–' She was unable to finish the sentence.

'I have done bad things, Elinor,' Lucius said heavily. 'I am no paragon.'

She smiled at him through her tears. 'I never thought you were.'

'I promise I would do anything to prevent you going through an experience like today's. Sir Hugo will have told you things about me. I can't claim that none of them are true. But I assure you that I have never, would never, hurt any lady – any woman.'

'Do you think I don't know that?' she asked, leaning her head on his shoulder.

'You still trust me? After everything?'

'I love you,' she said simply. 'Of course I trust you.' Elinor stood up and moved back onto the bed, holding her arms out to Lucius. 'Come here,' she said, 'and let me show you how much.'

'Elinor. Oh Elinor.'

Lucius lay beside her on the bed, kissing her over and over again. Every time he did, Elinor felt a jolt run through her, as if she had been caught by a gentle flash of lightning. She ran her fingers through his hair, then over his shoulders and back, pulling him closer still to her.

'My Lucius,' she murmured.

'All yours. Always yours,' he agreed between kisses.

'Show me,' she murmured, her fingers busy with the buttons on his shirt, even as her mouth sought his once more. 'Show me,' she said again, running fingers over his pale skin; stroking the muscular chest with new amazement. This, *this*, was all hers. Lucius was no one's but hers. How could an evening which had started in such fear and angst have ended here, in bed with the one man she had always loved? 'People say miracles don't happen,' she mumbled against his neck.

'I beg your pardon?'

She smiled. 'Nothing.'

She ran the tip of her tongue up his neck to his ear, and nibbled gently on the soft flesh of his lobe. He laughed, and squirmed against her; she could feel his hard erection pushing against her, and knew that she was desired.

'More,' she said; and Lucius laughed.

'That was what you said last time,' he reminded her.

'How you could think I did not enjoy it!' she replied, holding him as close as she could to her, revelling in the feeling of their bodies pressed together.

'Too many clothes,' Lucius complained. 'I want to feel your skin against mine.'

The very words set up an aching throb in Elinor. 'Yes. Oh yes.'

He moved away, and she made a small noise of complaint in her throat.

'I can't undress with you that close to me,' he teased.

His reminder about the last and only time they had made love came back to Elinor, and she sat up. 'Let me do it,' she urged.

'You?'

'Please?'

'The pleasure will be mine,' Lucius assured her. Then, more doubtfully, 'You are sure?'

'Surer than anything,' she said, helping him out of his jacket, and then undoing the remaining buttons on his shirt, kissing each new patch of skin as it appeared. 'Surer than anything at all,' she added as she pushed the shirt off, leaving him naked from the waist up. 'Oh Lucius, you're beautiful.' To her amazement, he blushed at this; Elinor did not think she had seen him embarrassed in his whole life before.

'That you should say that to me,' he said, his voice slightly hoarse.

She smiled up at him teasingly. 'I have no doubt I'm not the first,' she retorted. Then, placing another kiss against his chest, 'But I hope to be the last.'

'You are.'

Lucius might have said more, Elinor thought, but she had lowered her hands to his small-clothes, and he seemed to be finding it hard to breathe. Revelling in this power over her husband, she moved as slowly as she could bear to, tantalising him with her leisurely pace. His manhood jumped free as she pushed down his clothing, hard and begging for attention. She knelt down, took the very tip of the jutting erection into her mouth. Lucius groaned.

She pulled away. 'No?' she asked, knowing the answer.

'Yes,' he said, the word forced between his lips. 'Yes.'

She thought she could kneel there forever, between his legs, her mouth taking in the masculine flavour of his erection. She licked a line up towards the base, kissed him gently on her way back. He was wonderful – incredible. And he was hers. She could feel perspiration wetting her skin, drips slipping down between her cleavage and making her breasts tingle that little bit more. She wanted – she wanted everything. Perhaps they had the rest of their lives to do this, but she had already waited what seemed like a lifetime for Lucius. This time, she would have it all. This time, she would rejoice in every single second. No fear, no self-consciousness. Just pure physical love-making.

'Elinor. God, Elinor.' Lucius's words came out as if he could not help them; as if her name was all he had ever wanted to say. The tingling sensation grew within Elinor, not only in her breasts but lower down; in the places she had not even realised existed until Lucius had walked into her adult life, promising nothing and bringing her everything.

'You are wonderful,' she whispered; then, almost shyly despite herself, she took his manhood inside her mouth, sliding forward and allowing it to fill her. He was so long, so large, so incredibly wonderful. How could he ever have thought she did not worship his body? How could he ever have doubted her – doubted himself? She slid her mouth back and forth, back and forth, until there seemed to be no sensation in the world except for the feel of his erection sliding to and fro against her tongue, against the roof of her mouth. She would have given anything to take him in further, deeper, but her throat protested, and she preferred to keep him where she could taste him, taste every different secretion from his marvellous manhood.

She could have stayed like this forever, but Lucius sighed, pulling away with a reluctance that even Elinor could not doubt.

'No, beloved,' he murmured. 'I want to show you – I want to show you so much more.'

He hoisted her onto the bed and pushed the layers of her dress – petticoat – undershift up around her hips. The cloth bunched around her waist, and she wriggled impatiently to move it to more comfortable places. Lucius laughed.

'Oh yes,' he mumbled against her leg. 'Squirm like that for me, Elinor.'

'No.'

Her stubbornness returned for a second, and she lay still as a live woman can, just to provoke him. Their relationship never had been, despite his proposal, about obedience of a woman to a man, of Elinor to Lucius.

He smiled, and she could feel the movement of his lips against her thigh. 'Then I shall have to make you,' he said.

Elinor breathed out, her breath a hum of anticipation. She

could not – would not – tell him how much she hoped he would keep his promise. His warm breath tickled her skin; he placed kisses the length of one thigh then the other, but somehow it was the area in between which throbbed as his mouth touched her. Then, still gently, he brought his lips round to her centre, and trailed his tongue against ... Elinor bucked up against him as his tongue flickered against that spot of need between her thighs. He repeated the gesture again and again until she was moaning and pleading with him not to stop, to continue doing that – yes, *that*. And still he kept on, until there was a sudden unexpected rush of feeling, and Elinor cried out as the world exploded around her, leaving her hardly able to breathe, to move, to think. He pulled her into his arms and held her tight as she rode the waves of ecstasy.

'Lucius ...' When she could speak again, all she could think to say was his name. 'Lucius.'

'Yes, my Elinor?'

His erection stood proud and she wanted more, even now. She was wet and wanting and she reached a hand between his legs and guided him inside her, revelling at the sharp indrawn breath he took as his manhood pressed against her womanhood.

'I want you,' she said, her eyes fixed on his.

'Yes. Darling, yes.'

She rocked her hips back and forth, slowly, still keeping her gaze on him. There was a light pink flush against his cheeks and his eyes looked dark.

'Lucius.'

'So help me, Elinor, I can't be gentle if you keep doing that,' he murmured.

Her mouth twisted in a secretive smile as she continued to move. 'Maybe I don't want you to be.'

'Elinor, My God, Elinor, do you know how much I've dreamt of you like this?' Lucius's breathing was unsteady; and she laughed.

'Tell me.'

'I ...' Instead of speaking, however, he pushed her back against the bed and thrust into her time and time again. Elinor could sense that feeling building again – knew that it would not take long before she–

'*Lucius*,' she cried, the pleasure almost painful in its strength.

It seemed that was all he needed; she felt him pulse inside her as her heart thumped hard within her breast. There was a silence, a stillness, as they both tried to recover themselves. Then, as Lucius rolled onto his side and pulled her into his arms, Elinor spoke. 'You were right,' she said. 'I didn't think it could be better, but that was ...' She didn't have the words, but her smile said everything her words could not.

'Yes.' He kissed her. 'And next time will be better still.'

'I think I'll die,' she said, still smiling, 'but I'm prepared to risk it.'

Lucius laughed, and they were silent again for a moment. Then he spoke of what had happened before, his tone serious again.

'I will not challenge Sir Hugo,' he said, 'however much part of me wishes to. Duelling is for gentlemen, and Mansfield has proven himself anything but a gentleman. Also, I suspect this attack on you will be one of the last things Sir Hugo does before leaving the country. The man may not know it, but there is indignation afoot about bad gambling debts; and you are not the only lady whom he has discommoded.'

'I'm not sorry he is leaving,' Elinor replied, sober at once. 'And yet, in a strange sort of way I feel like thanking Sir Hugo. If it weren't for him, we might still be at cross purposes, still misunderstanding one another. And I'm gladdest of all that you won't challenge him. He does not deserve to have that power over our lives.'

He laughed. 'Most ladies would not be so generous, my

darling.'

'I'm not most ladies,' said Elinor, pulling Lucius tightly against herself again.

'No,' he said. He angled his head to look at her. 'No, you are not. You've never been "just another lady" to me, Elinor Crozier. I think you never will be.' And the fervour of the kiss he placed on her willing lips made her think he was right.

Safe Haven
by Shanna Germain

Chapter One

'YOU'RE FINE, YOU BIG lug. Quit your bitching.' Kallie kept
her voice soft and melodic, her tone a sweet-song of calm as
she moved around the big gelding, one hand holding tight to
his halter, the other making long, slow strokes along his
mottled grey neck.

Toddy didn't calm down much. Since he'd arrived at
Safe Haven two weeks ago, he hadn't quit any of his bad
habits, not the wood chewing or the nipping, not the nervous
prancing or the laid-back ears that were a clear threat to
whoever came near, but he'd stopped trying kill her, which
was an improvement. It had been a crazy couple of months.
Three new rescues, stress about money and keeping the farm
afloat, conversations with the bank, and, of course, ending
things with Erik. She thought he'd been the man of her
dreams – supporting her dream of a rescue farm, helping her
make payments on the land, even asking her to marry him –
but when she'd said no to the latter, he'd started pressuring
her to sell the land to him. Which was where she'd drawn
the line. She kind of missed having someone to help her out,
and she definitely missed the sex, but it was better to be
alone than to be with someone who wasn't right for her.
That's what her nana had always said.

In the meantime, if she did nothing more than stand here
brushing a nervous horse's trembling flank all day, showing

him that he was safe and loved, that was just fine with her. She swore the touch helped her as much as it did the animals. The farm, more than any other place, had always felt like home to her.

'Yes, it's your home now too,' she sing-songed to Toddy. 'Until you stop biting people, you big brat. Then we'll find you a nice place, with someone who loves you. Not like those jerks who left you to starve.'

Toddy leaned his ears back, not in threat but to listen to her voice, and Kallie rewarded him with a bit more crooning.

That was the secret to working with animals, Kallie had discovered a long time ago. You could say whatever you wanted as long as you said it in the right voice. It was all about making them feel safe and loved. And most of the animals who ended up at Safe Haven, animals like Toddy, whose owners had left him locked in a barn for weeks with no food or water, they needed to feel cared for most of all.

'You're doing great, Big Guy,' she said. Letting go of Toddy's halter, Kallie slipped half a carrot from her pocket and held it out on her flat palm. Toddy eyed her with his big brown eyes. It always broke her heart a little when an animal was so scared they didn't even come for treats. She kept herself still, willing him to come and take it from her, willing him to trust her enough to take the risk.

Down by the road, the other horses – six of them, all rescues like Toddy – neighed, one by one. She often joked about them being the farm's warning system, but it wasn't really a joke. They only neighed like that if a strange vehicle was coming up the driveway. And strangers were never a good thing at Safe Haven. It either meant an animal needed rescue or her Erik had sent one of his hired hands to try to talk her into selling the land. Again.

So much for her tiny moment of peace.

'Shit,' she swore, her tone sounding as grumpy as she felt.

In response, Toddy snorted and stamped his foot, throwing his head in the air, showing the whites of his eyes.

'Sorry, big boy,' she said, her voice almost back to its soft croon. 'You lucked out this time. Me, not so much.'

She held out the carrot for another moment, hoping that the visitor would go away or that Toddy would come and take the treat from her. But he stayed in the corner with his ears back and the horses kept up their doorbell neighs. Sighing, she left the carrot in Toddy's feed bin, then slipped out of the stall and went to greet whatever fresh hell was arriving on her doorstep.

It wasn't one of the Eric's hired hands. And it wasn't, at least as far as she could tell, a new rescue animal. And if it was fresh hell, it was incredibly sexy fresh hell in jeans and black boots. A fresh hell of a tall, curly haired man pushing a motorcycle up her gravel drive. As he walked, the horses were following him, keeping as close to the fence line as they could, tossing their heads and snorting at him.

A second later, she realised they weren't snorting at the man. They were snorting at the wriggling bundle of fur that was bounding up the driveway after him. Great. So it *was* a random drop off. She wanted to stop them right there and tell them that Safe Haven was full. She didn't have time or room for any more strays. Not even cute strays. Especially not cute strays. She had enough trouble on her hands.

But her voice, which had so recently been crooning at a huge horse, now seemed stuck in her throat.

'Hey there!' the man called as he got closer. He raised one hand off the motorcycle in something like a wave. He wore a thick silver ring on his middle finger, and her eyes were drawn first to its glint, and then to his long fingers and strong wrists, then to the length of his bare arm, the lightly tanned bicep that was offset by the blue fabric of his T-shirt. 'Are you Kallie?'

She started to say no, even though she knew it wouldn't

do any good; someone had obviously sent him, even though everyone knew Safe Haven didn't rescue dogs or cats, and it definitely didn't rescue beautiful, curly haired men with motorcycles and fantastic smiles. But she started to deny her birth name anyway, because this was trouble walking up her driveway. She could feel it. Even the horses could feel it.

Then he lifted up his sunglasses, pushing them up on his head and any words she might have said completely disappeared.

He had blue eyes. Not just blue eyes, but poppy-blue eyes. Fall-into-a-dream blue eyes. Sky on the first day of summer blue. Almost surreal in their bright gaze, surrounded by small wrinkles as he gazed at her. She heard her own sharp intake of breath and felt stupid for its sound in the mostly quiet day.

'Kallie, right?' he asked.

She nodded. Look away from his eyes, she thought. Just ... look anywhere elsc. But she couldn't. They were so blue, threaded with silver that shone funny in the sunlight.

'Oh, good,' he said. He looked away – she was so grateful for being released from his gaze that she could hear her heart thumping in her chest – and kicked his bike stand to settle it on the gravel. Then, he bent down and picked up the wriggling bundle of fur that had been stalking his boot laces.

In contrast to the man's intense blue eyes, the puppy's curious brown gaze was a hundred times easier to take. His tongue lolling to the side, he settled into the man's arms and gave a happy yip. The puppy licked his fingers, and the man gave a quick, delighted laugh.

Kallie's heart did something funny in her chest. She stuck her hand in her pocket, realised she still had half a carrot in there, and pulled her hand out quickly, trying to wipe the wet off on her jeans without being obvious.

The man didn't seem to notice her movements. He reached for the puppy's single white paw and made it move

140

up and down in the semblance of a wave.

'Hi, I'm Gauntlet,' the man said, his voice a growled approximation of a puppy voice. Kallie choked back laughter, and ended up just coughing in the process.

'Are you OK?'

'Fine,' she said after a moment, although she clearly wasn't. She was the world's biggest dork. She cleared her throat, and finally found her voice. 'But ... Gauntlet?'

The man looked at the puppy in his arms as though he'd just seen him for the first time. Then the man smiled. Dimples. Wrinkles. Oh sweet heaven. She was in so much trouble. She thought her libido had dried up after Erik left – an event her friend Shar called the Double B, "the Big Breakup" – but clearly that wasn't true. *Go back to the barn, girl. Now. Before you get yourself in more trouble.*

'I've been calling him Gauntlet. You know, for the glove. Also ...' the man leaned toward her and whispered, covering the puppy's ears with one hand. 'Because he's kind of skinny. Like, Gaunt. But I didn't tell him that part. Didn't want him to feel bad.'

'Uh.' Kallie had no idea what to do with this. A man who named a puppy after a piece of armour, but who also covered his ears while saying something that might hurt his feelings. She felt like she was standing on uneven ground, something that threatened to cave away under her if she moved so much as a single step. Now she thought she knew how the animals felt, coming here, their whole lives changing in a sudden, quick shift.

The man's cheeks pinked a little, just along the tops of his curved cheekbones, and he shrugged, lifting wide shoulders beneath the sleeves of his T-shirt. 'Silly, I know. But I had to call him something. I found him abandoned on the side of the road. Down on ... I forget, that stretch that follows the river.'

'Sharpsteen,' she said automatically. He didn't know where he was. Which meant he wasn't from around here.

Just passing through on his way to wherever he belonged. She was safe. However sexy this man was – and he *was* sexy in all the right ways for her, she could admit that now – he wasn't going to stay. He wasn't going to ask her to give up the thing she loved. He wasn't going to shake her world up and send her spinning.

'The fire chief told me you take strays,' he said.

'Bill told you that, did he?' Hmph. She would have to "thank" him for that later. If her best friend's husband wasn't trying to set her up with one of his fire deputies, it appeared he was sending stray ... creatures her way.

'He did,' the man said.

That smile again. Oh, for the love of God. Who was allowed to have both blue eyes and a smile like that? It wasn't right. Transient or not, she wasn't going to let him get any closer than this. He could take his motorcycle and his cute bundle of fur right back down the driveway back to wherever they'd come from.

'No, uh ... puppies,' Kallie said. She tried to keep the tremor from her voice, but mostly failed. It came through loud and clear, a little squeak of something. What the hell was wrong with her? She swallowed and tried again. 'I don't take puppies. But I can get you the number of the shelter if you like. Come into the barn.'

Where had that come from? What about him going back down the driveway on the bike he rode in on? Everyone knew you weren't supposed to ask a total stranger into your barn. Not even – no, especially not – a stranger who was sexy six ways to Sunday, with cerulean eyes that just about knocked her out. A stranger with a fantastic smile, and the potential for a fantastic laugh, if his response to the puppy was any indication. And that was just as dangerous for her right now. No relationships, no sex. That's what she'd promised herself after Erik had left. Just her and Safe Haven.

Except that suddenly Safe Haven didn't feel all that safe

any more, did it?

She hoped he'd say no to her to offer.

Instead, he said, 'That would be great.' And started in the direction of the barn without her.

He had long legs and a longer stride, and she felt herself nearly running to catch up with him. The barn door was still open, where she'd left it. He stepped inside and Kallie followed, the scent of hay and horse hide filling her nose as it always did. Home, she thought, as she always did, and took a moment to let it swirl around her and fill her.

Toddy bent his long neck to peer through the wide slats of his stall, snorting his alarm at the strange man and the even stranger bundle he was carrying.

Trust me, I know how you feel, big boy. Kallie laid a hand on the stall to remind Toddy she was there, that she had everything under control. It didn't help; Toddy stamped his forefoot against the stall, as though to tell her what she already knew: nothing about this was under control.

Oblivious, the man bent toward the rabbit hutches hanging from the wall. 'Cute,' he said, conversationally, as the farm's resident rabbits – two white angoras – came bounding forward, ears high, putting their fuzzy paws on the wire in the hopes of getting treats. Traitors, she thought. I bring a cute guy in here once and you're all over him, despite the fact he's even got a puppy in his arms.

He bent down farther, the pup still wigging in the crook of one arm, and held out a finger to the rabbits' noses. His jeans did that wonderful thing that jeans do, where they hugged the good curves of ass and thigh, and it took her a moment to realise that she wasn't just *noticing*. She was *staring*. At his ass.

She turned away, blinking. What was wrong with her? If he'd turned around and seen her doing that ...

'I have the number in here, give me a second,' she said as she began digging through the desk drawer where she kept farm odds and ends.

'Why don't you take puppies?' he asked, turning away from the rabbits to face her.

She'd found the number and was tearing off a piece of paper to write it down. Digging for a pen. Trying not to look at him, mainly.

'What?' she asked.

'Why no puppies?'

It took her a moment to remember, and in that second she forgot her promise not to look at him. 'Because someone else will.'

He gave her a questioning look. She looked down at the puppy, unwilling or unable to meet his gaze again. Reaching out to touch the pup's ears, she stopped herself halfway. Don't touch, she thought. But on the heels of that, her passing glimpse at his hands revealed a tiny tattoo: a single word written across the top outside of his pointer finger. She couldn't read the cursive, the letters cut off by one of the puppy's paws.

'Someone else will what?' he asked.

'Take puppies,' she said. 'They're cute and young, so they're easy to find a home for. He'll get snapped up before you can say a proper goodbye.'

How true that was. In so many ways.

At her words, she could have sworn he hugged the puppy tighter to his chest. His lovely, wide, oh-my-God-stop-looking chest. That lovely flat space hidden beneath fabric and arms and puppy.

'Why don't *you* want to keep him?' she asked.

'It's complicated.'

Of course it was. Handsome guys who walked up your driveway holding cute puppies were always complicated.

'I'm sorry,' he said suddenly. 'I just realised I don't even know your name. I'm Darrin, Darrin Daughtery.'

Handsome guys with unusual names who walked up your driveway were even more complicated.

'Kallie Peters,' she said, and it was almost a whisper,

144

caught in there, unwilling to come out.

The silence stretched between them. He was looking at her, really looking, like he either wanted to paint her or steal her away. She couldn't tell which. It was uncomfortable, under that beautiful blue gaze, but it was also like being lifted somewhere high and pure. Appreciated. Seen. With a suddenness that surprised her, she had a mental image of him, naked next to her, looking over at her with that same intense expression, his fingers following the curves of her body, teasing lightly before they grew stronger and reached to push her thighs open ...

'Is that for me?' he asked.

For one brief, bright moment, she thought he meant her. Or something of her.

Then she remembered the piece of paper in her hand. Right. She was supposed to be getting him out of here, not inviting him in. 'The number of the shelter,' she said. 'And the directions. It's only a few minute's drive. Or, bike, in your case.'

She held the paper out by its very corner, giving him lots of room to take it. She wasn't going to touch his absolutely adorable puppy. She wasn't going to touch him. She wasn't.

Darrin leaned forward to take the paper. She could feel the heat of his body, hear the puppy's soft breath. They were that close. Darrin's back to Toddy's stall. Her back to the open door. Only the wriggling puppy and a little bit of air between them. Air that was suddenly becoming hard for Kallie to catch hold of in her body.

He came toward her. For a second, a tiny split second, her brain thought he meant to kiss her and her body reacted as though her brain was right, her lips doing that thing they did before a kiss, the sense of anticipation slivering through her stomach like cool water.

And then Darrin was howling, shoving the puppy into her chest. She had no choice but to open her arms and take the wriggling creature into her grasp and hold it tight, letting it

145

lick her face. Even as the strange man in her barn started swearing at her, his yells scaring even the rabbits to the very backs of their cages.

Chapter Two

KALLIE PETERS WAS THE most beautiful thing Darrin had
ever seen. And he'd spent a lot of time around beauty in his
time as an LA fashion photographer. Men and women with
perfect proportions and the kind of hair and faces that took
hours or sometimes even days, the kind of beauty that drew
the eye to it with a kind of magic, but which was as false as
the people inside it. He'd never seen anyone who looked as
naturally ... alive as this woman did. She'd stepped out of
the barn in her dark jeans and butter yellow tank top, her
hair lifting off her neck in the slight wind, and the first thing
he'd thought was that Gauntlet had just peed on him. A
second later, he realised, gratefully, that it was just the heat
in his chest from watching her walk toward him.

He'd got used to talking aloud to the puppy and he nearly
did so now, but caught himself just before his lips moved.
So he kept up the banter in his head instead.

*Please don't pee on me in front of this woman, G.
Promise me, and I promise to let you lick the grease from
my fingers next time I have bacon.*

The puppy, content in Darrin's arms, had merely raised a
baby puppy eyebrow without a sound and waggled his little
white paw

Darrin took that as a yes.

Either way, Gauntlet hadn't peed on him, not one little
bit. And Kallie had invited him into her beautiful barn and
he'd wanted nothing more than to touch the curl that kept
escaping next to her ear. To make her laugh. To look into
her hazel eyes, the way the green was split with little rays of

yellow that reminded him of the woods on a sunlit day. To lean in and press his lips to hers, to see if she tasted as alive as she looked.

He'd been so close to that last one.

Then that belligerent beast of a horse had stuck his face through the slats of his pen and bitten the back of his calf right through his jeans, and now the most beautiful woman in the world was kneeling at his feet. Which would have been hot as hell if he wasn't in screaming pain and she wasn't pressing a bag of frozen raspberries to the back of his leg. He was afraid to look at the damage and, despite the fact that the pain was making him feel a little woozy, he was content just to look at her instead. She was the perfect distraction. The strap of her tank top had slipped to the side, revealing a tiny bit of pale skin that he couldn't stop looking at. It looked like cream, like meringue. He could just feel the tips of her hair brushing his jeans, and he found himself almost sad that the horse had bitten a place she could access without removing his pants

'I'm so sorry,' she was saying. 'He's new. He was really, really in bad shape when I got him. I've been working with him, but ... God, I'm just so sorry.' She was babbling in a cute kind of way, the pinks of her cheeks flushed lightly as she pressed the bag at what felt like random spots to his calf, making his head swim with cold and pain.

She pulled the makeshift icepack off his skin, touched a spot with his finger. He let out half a yelp before he stopped himself, forcing the sound into something more manly.

Gauntlet, who'd been amusing himself by chewing on something that Kallie had given him, perked his ears as Kallie began to laugh quietly.

'I'm sorry,' she said, between giggles. He could tell she was trying very hard to be serious, but the edges of her mouth twitched every time she closed her lips between words and the corners of her eyes were all wrinkled up. 'It's just ... you're fine, but you have Toddy's dental records on the back of your calf.'

'Seriously?' he asked.

'Look for yourself,' she said.

The throbbing in his leg told him that he didn't really need to look. That he probably shouldn't look. Pain he could handle, even if it did make him sound like a rabbit in a trap. Blood was OK too. But the sensation in his calf told him it was already turning the colour of grape jelly and swelling to at least twice its normal size, and that was something he did not need to see.

'I'll pass,' he said.

'Big baby,' she said, glancing up at him from the corner of her eye. The tease and that flash of her honeyed eyes made his chest do that warm, puppy-pee thing again. 'He didn't even break the skin.'

'I liked you better when you were apologising,' he said, but even through his pain, he couldn't keep the tease from his voice. She had handled the whole thing with such calm coolness that he'd found himself first surprised, then impressed. Although why he was surprised, he didn't know. If she could handle all of these animals and herself, it made sense that she'd be able to handle a situation in which a stranger walked into her barn and was brought to his knees by the dental records of an equine.

She pressed the icepack back against his skin, and he ground his teeth against the yelp that threatened to follow, pushing it into a soft curse instead. Who knew a horse bite could hurt so much and not even need stitches? Not that he wanted stitches. But still, it would make it easier to explain the very unmanly like yelps he made every time she shifted. It would also make it easier to explain the reaction that her presence was having, the way he had to move away slightly every time she leaned against him, or brushed him with her hair or her breasts or even just her elbow. He'd noticed the sensation the first time her hair had fallen around his thighs, and he'd had a sudden image of her naked and kneeling, her

149

hand around his cock. He'd felt the shift, the half-hardening and felt like his cock was betraying him; how could it react at a moment like this?

'Here, can you hold it for a second?' When she asked it, he was still thinking about his cock and her fingers, and it took him a moment to realise she meant the ice pack. He leaned down carefully to press the frozen bag against his leg, trying not to wince. 'Thanks. Now that you no longer look like you're about to pass out, I'm just going to call the vet real quick.'

'The what?' The strain of speaking made his head swim a little, and he lowered his voice. 'The horse is fine. *He* bit *me*. It's not like I'm going to bite him back.'

'The vet is for you.'

She flashed him that grin again, half-sweet and half-wicked. For the first time since he'd started this cross-country motorcycle tour, he wished he had his camera. He wanted to capture that expression, the way her eyes darkened, the green deepening as the yellow flared.

'Trust me,' she said. 'You're better off with Shar than with the doctors around here. Besides, she's cheaper. And she can check out your puppy while she's at it.'

She unhooked the receiver from a yellow rotary phone that looked like it had been in the barn for a long, long time. Before she dialled, she turned to him, and her voice, while attempting for playful, fell far short of it, her smile faltering. 'I just want to make sure you're OK. I'll cover the vet costs, and whatever else you need. I can't afford a lawsuit. I'm really sorry.'

Hearing that, Darrin felt the need not just to reassure her, but oddly to protect her. He didn't know from what, and the pain in his calf was making it hard to think. If he'd been able to stand up and reach her, he would have hugged her close. Which probably would have earned him another bite – this time from a pissed-off farm owner instead of said farm owner's horse. Probably a good thing he couldn't get up.

'I'm not going to sue you,' was the best he could come up with.

She didn't respond, but through the pain, he could hear her talking on the phone. He leaned back against the wall, closing his eyes. This was not what he'd expected to find when he'd left San Francisco for a month-long trip around the country. He'd expected to find the open road. He'd expected him alone on the bike for miles and miles, for days at a time. He'd *hoped* to find his creativity again once he'd left behind the day-to-day work of shooting stuck-up models who all looked the same.

What he wasn't expecting was to find an abandoned puppy by the side of the road. Or this adorable woman with her amazing curves and her intense gaze. And lust? Desire? A half-hard cock throbbing almost as much as the pain in his leg? That wasn't even something that had been on his radar. And yet, here he was, unable to stand and in serious pain, still wanting to open his eyes just enough to see what the woman in front of him was doing, to see the curves of her delicious ass as she walked around in the slanted sunlight and the hay chaff.

Kallie hung up the phone and came toward him, holding out two blue pills on her palm. 'Shar will be here shortly. She said to take one of these.'

'Let me guess? Horse tranquilizer?' It was a running joke on the set, something the models always said if someone got nervous and asked them if they'd eaten. Horse tranqs for breakfast.

Kallie canted her head at him. 'Noooo. Those would involve sticking you in the ass with a needle. Which I can do if you like. These, however, are just Midol.'

'Midol?' This was getting worse and worse. Whatever lust he might feel for this woman was clearly not going to make a difference. She'd seen him get bit, heard him squealing in pain and was now offering him pills for PMS.

She tucked the pills into his palm. 'They do wonders for

swelling. You'd be surprised.'

He took them, coughing a little at their size, and then leaned back against the barn wall. Kallie was kneeling at his feet again, and he tried to push away the new images that her movement brought: her, looking up at him with those gorgeous green eyes while she swirled her tongue around the tip of his cock, dragged her lips up the sensitive veins along the underside ... That was a mental image that made him want to take photos again. And fuck. God, how long had he been alone, with nothing between his legs but a motorcycle? Far too long.

He could feel Kallie taking the ice pack from his hands, rolling his pant leg higher up, her fingers cool against his skin, her breath heating the places her touch had just cooled. How could one have pain and pleasure at the same time? He didn't know, but he felt he could sit there forever, letting her touch him and soothe him ... He let the daydream come, only because it wouldn't stay away and he was already hard beneath the tightening pull of his jeans, Kallie licking her lips and lowering her mouth over his cock, slow so he could watch her take the whole thing in, his hands fisting in her hair, knowing by the heat in her eyes that she was enjoying it as much as she was.

'I think he'll live.' A voice he didn't know, something slightly off about it. Not an accent but ...

He opened his eyes and realised he'd been, maybe not dozing, but definitely not all there. Or maybe he had been dozing, because it was no longer Kallie at his feet, but someone else. Strawberry blonde hair pulled back in a ponytail, and then the face lifted and he was looking into a pair of dark hazel eyes full of amusement. An odd-shaped stethoscope with an electronic box on it rested around her neck.

'So, I was just telling Kallie that we'll have to take off your leg,' the woman said. Her words were slightly clipped, but easy enough to understand. 'But other than that, you'll be fine.'

'What?' he asked. He felt suddenly awake, the pain in his leg amplified. 'No, wait, what ...?'

'Kidding,' she said. 'Kallie, I thought you said he had a ...'

The woman turned away from him, her fingers flying as she faced Kallie. Kallie answered back, her fingers moving just as quickly. Suddenly, he understood the unusual sound of her voice. She was deaf. Or partly deaf? He didn't even know that someone who had hearing loss could be a doctor. Or, in this case, a vet.

The two women laughed together, and then returned their attention to him.

'Shar, Darrin. Darrin, Shar. Oh, and that's Gauntlet,' Kallie said, pointing to the puppy who was sleeping under one of the rabbit hutches.

Shar cocked her head. 'Oh, you're the stray my husband found.' She was looking at the puppy, but Darrin got the impression she was talking about him.

'Your husband is the fire chief?' Small town. He'd forgotten how those worked. Everyone knew everyone or was married to someone's brother or engaged to or ... Which made him wonder whether Kallie was attached. She hadn't said anything, but then they'd barely got a conversation in before, well, this.

'You're going to be fine,' Shar said. 'He didn't break the skin, and he's got all his shots. I'm going to give you something for the pain, and I think you should stay here and rest for a couple of days so I can come back and check on you. That calf's going to be too sore to ride with anyway, plus the meds. I'll give Gauntlet his first round of shots, too. He'll be sleepy for the rest of the day. More so than usual. You too, probably. I'm sure Kallie can take good care of you both.'

At that, Kallie responded with a flow of fast fingers that

was clearly a curse of some sort, which brought laughter to Darrin's lips. Something was happening between the two women, but he couldn't tell what. He guessed they'd been friends for a long time, not just from the way they teased each other, but with their ability to switch communication tactics. It was like watching twins with a secret language.

The fingers flew, until Shar took Kallie's wrists in her hands and held her still.

'Don't argue with the doctor,' Shar said. 'Nor with your best friend. One of us always wins.'

Chapter Three

FOR A DAY OR two. Kallie sighed. Damn Shar – she knew Darrin was just fine to leave. Just as Bill had known Safe Haven didn't take puppies. And yet there was currently both a man and a puppy sitting in her living room, looking at her expectantly.

Sighing, Kallie made the puppy a place to sleep – a pillow, a stuffed bunny that Shar had found in her vet van and that he'd latched on to fast, plus a couple of old bowls for food and water. Last, she wound up an old alarm clock and tucked the ticking machine under the pillow.

'It'll sound like a heartbeat,' she told Gauntlet. In turn, he gave her a puppy face lick, smelling of sunshine and dog food.

'Puppy seal of approval,' Darrin said. When she turned, he was standing one-footed in the hallway, leaning against the doorjamb.

'I have a feeling it's going to last until I leave the room and that's about it.'

'He hasn't made a peep the couple of nights I've had him.'

'And he slept where?'

Darrin had the smarts to at least flash her a sheepish grin. 'Well, kind of near me.'

'As in, on your pillow?'

'If I say no, will you believe it?' God that smile again. It was like it zoomed across the room every time he flashed it, hit her hard in the chest and then zoomed down between her legs. It made her feel like she was the one hobbling around instead of him.

'You can sit, you know.' He did so, releasing an involuntary oof that made her realise just how much in pain he actually was. Even sitting there, even in pain, she liked the way he looked in her living room. He'd pulled his dark curls back into a low, short ponytail that showed off the angle of his jaw, the strong line of his neck. She wondered what he would smell like, if she were to tuck her face into the crook of his shoulder.

In the kitchen, the coffee maker hissed its ready warning and she poured two cups. She handed over one of the mugs, their fingers just touching around the cup. She felt it all the way to her wrists and up into her chest. Damn.

'Hungry?' she asked, retreating to the doorway. 'I can cook something.' Something else to occupy her. A way to keep busy. What else was she going to do with this man in her living room? Besides try desperately to stop looking at him.

He shook his head. 'Not in the least.'

Kallie curled her hands around the cup. 'Sorry about Shar. She can be a pain.'

'I liked her,' he said. It seemed like a genuine comment. Beneath that, she could clearly hear his unspoken question.

'She's only fully deaf in one ear, partly in the other,' she said. 'She reads lips like a motherfucker, though. Mostly when you don't want her to.'

'And the signing?' he asked.

'The doctors were sure she was going to go fully deaf before she was an adult. We kind of learned together. It's a bastardized version, though. No one else understands it.'

It was easy to talk about Shar, it gave her something to think about besides him sitting on her couch with his easy posture. His long fingers wrapped around the mug. Those blue eyes which seemed, impossibly, to be getting brighter and bluer as afternoon slipped into evening.

'Thank you for letting me stay here,' he said. 'I

feel ... like a ...' He dipped his head to sip at his coffee.

'I don't even know what you're doing here.' It was out before she meant it to be, before she thought it through. 'I mean ...' she started. Shit, what did she mean? She meant she wanted to know everything: where he'd come from, what he was on his way to, whether he would stay just for a little while to strip her down and kiss the lonely parts of her body. If the answer to that was yes, that he would stay and then go, she thought she could let her guard down, invite him in. But she didn't even know how to ask it.

'I know what you mean,' he said, and she thought he actually might.

'What *are* you doing here?' she asked.

Darrin seemed to consider this. 'I'm a photographer, in LA. I got burnt out. My photos were getting ... stale. So I took a little time to ride around the country. See if I could find my, I don't know ...' He looked at her, that clear blue gaze steady and strong, the weight of it sending her desire up through her thighs, into the heat of her cheeks. '...passion again.'

Kallie returned the gaze as long as she could, savouring the stream of lust through her body, and then she lowered her head to stare at the surface of her coffee. 'So you're only passing through?'

'Yes,' he said. And suddenly, 'I'd like to touch you.'

The words, the ease with which he'd said them, the strength, and his bright blue gaze as it fell on her, all of it made her feel unsteady again, as if gravity was changing its laws every second.

'Nice segue,' she said, trying to keep things light, refusing to admit the impact he was having on her.

He laughed, shook his head, setting his coffee on the table. 'I feel stupid, like this. Not being able to get up and come to you, to make the first move, but, well ...' He waved a hand at his calf, the pant leg still rolled up to his knee, the swelling visible from where she stood.

'So you're saying you'd like me to make the first move?' Her smile surprised her; it felt sleek and sly. What was she doing? She held her cup tighter, as though that might stop the words from coming out, or stop the tumbling, falling lust that filled her stomach.

'I'm saying I'd like someone to make the first move,' he said. 'And sadly, I'm clearly not up to it.'

'Well, that could be a problem, don't you think?' She toyed with her coffee cup, hearing the tease in her own voice, feeling both excited and embarrassed by its obviousness. So much for not touching him. For not letting him touch her.

'Please come here and kiss me,' he said.

No one had ever asked her please like that before; no one had ever asked anything so simple. He wasn't asking for permission, nor if she was interested. Instead, he was laying his desire out there so clearly and asking her to help him reach it. She'd never known anyone so quietly confident, so willing to ask for what he wanted.

Her mind, that last bastion of safe choices, shut off all its alarm systems as his request. Her body, already willing and wanting, helped her put the cup on the table without spilling it, and go to him. She thought she'd feel nervous or awkward making the first move. Instead, the closer she got, the more her body seemed to know what to do, how to settle itself near him without touching his injured calf, how to put herself where she needed to be in order to do the thing she'd been wanting to do since he first walked up her driveway: kiss him.

She settled herself on the couch, then leaned in and touched her lips to his. He opened his mouth, releasing a sigh of sound and want, the taste of his lips like fall wind and apples, like fresh cider, a taste she could drink up forever if he'd let her. She felt her body melt against him, the heat of his chest, the rough of his jeans, the way his arm reaching around her without hesitation to pull her closer. His curls fell around their faces, soft enough to nearly tickle, and she giggled against his mouth.

'What?' he asked, pulling away from her without going anywhere, leaving them touching nose-to-nose, his eyes still closed, his breath soft, quick exhales warmed her face.

'Tickled,' she said. 'Do it again.'

He obliged, canting his head to find her mouth with his. She sucked his bottom lip, running her teeth over the flesh softly, then released her tease as his tongue found hers, joining her. He sunk his hand into her hair, pulling it from its ponytail to run his fingers through it, his grip light at first, tightening as they sunk deeper into the kiss. Kallie shifted, her body aching to be closer to his, to press fully against him.

'Ow,' he said, but it was a sound lost in their kissing, half-buried in the heat and press of their mouths.

A second later, he took her by the shoulders, pushing her away from him. She made a little sound, like a whine, and then clapped her hand over her mouth, laughing through her palm. 'Sorry.'

'No, no,' he said. 'It's good. It's just ... do you think we could ... I'd like to do any number of very, very dirty things to you,' he said. The blunt words, combined with the gentle sweep of his thumb along her jawline, made her shiver. 'However, the couch is ... do you have a bed?'

'No,' she said.

This time it was her turn to delight at the expression on his face. She suddenly understood why Shar loved to tease people so much.

'Brat,' he said.

'Probably,' she admitted.

'Well, I'd love to see it.'

'OK,' she said.

'Um ... You have to get off me if you want me to get up.'

'Hmm. Dilemmas.'

He slipped his hands beneath her ass and lifted her in a

single quick move. She felt the strength of his arms as he did so, the muscles from motorcycle riding and whatever else he did. She realised she didn't even know what he did, but she didn't care either. She had to close her eyes against the wave of want that rushed through her. Was there nothing about this man that didn't turn her on? It was something that should have sent all her warning bells ringing into overdrive, but it didn't. And that scared her even more.

Yet it didn't stop her from asking if he needed a hand off the couch, knowing even as she did so that there was only one place they were going from there.

He let her help him up, his weight a heavy, solid press against her shoulders as they made their way down her short hallway. It amazed her that he was half crippled, leaning on a woman half his size, unable to walk, and still he wore his confidence like a perfectly tailored suit. He wasn't apologetic, he wasn't putting on his man vibes in an attempt to make himself look better. She'd forgotten that there were men like that; maybe she *had* been living in this small town too long.

They made their way slowly, him half-hopping on one foot.

'Good thing it's only one floor,' she said, her breath huffing slightly under his weight.

'Right. If you had to carry me upstairs, I doubt you'd have any energy left for sex. Probably have to take a nap first.'

'Who says we're having sex?'

'That kiss back there says we're having sex. Unless I decide not to, of course.'

'I could drop you, you know,' she said.

His laugh was deep and warm, his arm tightening around her in a way that was nearly possessive. Her body responded instantly, the prickle of her nipples sending little sparks through her. Oh, hell. She was in far more than just a bit of trouble this time.

160

By the time they made it to the bedroom, she was sweating a little. Not the sexiest thing ever, but she had a feeling it was more from the proximity than from the exertion. And he didn't seem to mind. At the doorway, he turned her so she faced him, buried his hands into her hair and lifted her face to his, kissing the curve of her chin, her jawline, and finally her lips. He did it over and over, without seeming to hurry or press, and yet she found she was panting, arcing into his touch, aware that he was standing on one foot, but barely caring. It had been far too long since she'd had someone touch her, since she'd found herself letting go, getting lost in a simple feeling like pleasure.

Darrin was proud that he made it all the way down the hallway without hobbling too much, even though the pain in his calf yelled at him with every step. Her bedroom was simple and clean, yet with touches that showed it to be fully hers, just like the barn. The fabrics were deep maroons and butter yellows, dark greens. It was like the simplest garden. Even in the fading light, he was torn between wanting to lay her down naked on the bed and ravage her, and wanting to lay her down naked on the bed and take a thousand photos of her. He'd been imagining what her curves looked like beneath her simple jeans, beneath the tank top. Now, he'd had a chance to feel some of them and he wanted more and more.

He kissed her, slow and sweet, the kind of kisses he liked best, the kind he'd missed in the wham-bam world of model photography. No pressure, no expectation, just a chance to linger in her scent and flavour, in the soft heat of her body. And her hair, God, he could touch her hair forever. Natural and soft, free-flowing, just perfect for sinking his hands into, for holding her against him. And she seemed to like it, which made him like it even more.

He moved them slowly toward the bed and laid her down on the spread – for someone so strong, she was surprisingly light – and then he lowered his body down beside her. The ache in his calf was still there, but seemed to be receding. He wasn't sure whether if it was because the pain pills were working or because something in Kallie's presence, her touch, made him notice it less.

He rolled against her, savouring the curves of her body beneath her jeans, the soft spill of her waist and hips. She laughed beneath him, sweet and strong, her body meeting his in all the right places with a carefree ease.

The bit of skin, that white strip beneath her tank top strap was peeking out again, and he leaned forward and kissed it, running his tongue over the smooth cream of her. She tasted like fresh sweat and sweet clover, salt and honey. He sucked her skin into his mouth, hearing her moan softly in response.

A second later, she gave a laugh, the kind that he was learning to savour even before it happened, the kind he knew he could learn to look forward to, and then she was saying, 'What are you waiting for?' in his ear, soft and sweet, a bit of breath and want that made him so hard he felt achy over it.

The laugh lines around her eyes were tiny indents of skin and he traced them with a couple of fingers, feeling her lashes against his skin. He bit her ear, the very bottom where her earring rested, tasting metal and skin. 'I'm waiting for you to undress me,' he said. 'Because I'm sick and all.'

'You're not sick.' But her fingers, delightfully, were already finding his hips, his jeans, opening the snaps, searching in a ticklish way for the parts of him he most wanted her to touch. He pulled her tank top over her head even as she was trying to tug his jeans over his hips. Getting naked with her was a crazy, wild thing, hair and fingers and him saying, 'wait, wait,' as he gingerly pulled the fabric over his throbbing calf. Soon, he was on her bed in nothing but his boxers, while she stretched out beside him, minus only her tank top. Her bra was simple, black and touched with lace only at the very edges. Her nipples, hard pink peaks, pushed the fabric out. He reached for the front-clasp, wanting to watch it fall open, hungering to take her nipples into his mouth and suckle them until she was moaning and writhing.

She intercepted his hand with a reach of her own.

'Boxers,' she said. 'Nice. But nicer off.'

Her cool fingers exploring him gave him a new sound, something somewhere between a word and a groan, and every time he made it, she tightened her grip lightly, pleasantly, as if urging him forward. She kissed him again, letting her mouth trail over his jawline, into the curve of his neck, using both and on the length of his cock, wrapping them and tugging in soft, slow strokes that made him yearn to be inside her.

He ducked his head, slipping the top edge of her bra down, taking one of her nipples into his mouth. It hardened against his tongue, a soft sensitive peak that he couldn't get enough of. And the way her body responded – he'd never known anyone who was so in her body, so present, responding to every touch and tease. That alone made him almost as hard as her movements over his cock.

He wanted to know if the rest of her responded that way, if he could pull that much pleasure from her elsewhere.

'Wait,' he tried. 'Why am ... I the only one fully naked?' His words were puffs of sound between the strokes of her hands, stilted and groaned.

'Dunno,' she said. 'You could do something about–'

She stopped suddenly, both words and hands going still, lifting her head from the bed to glance out the bedroom window.

'Wh–?' he started.

'Shhh ...' And a second later, 'Shit.'

She bounded from bed, pulling on her tank top, watching out the bedroom window with a serious expression on her face. He followed her gaze to where a black pickup was pulling up the driveway.

'Damn him,' she said. 'Stay here.'

And then she left him there, naked, throbbing, wanting, hard as hell and more than a little confused.

Chapter Four

ERIK WAS GETTING OUT of the truck by the time Kallie made it outside. He'd taken to shaving his blond hair and wearing cowboy hats lately, and so when he turned to her, his face was entirely in shadow.

'What are you doing here?' she asked. Even though she knew full well. It was like the only thing that would come out of her mouth when she saw him. She crossed her arms over her chest, and realised she smelled strongly like sex. Or almost sex. Which made her think of Darrin, left back there in her bed, probably totally freaking out. Damn. Double damn.

'Hey Kal.' Erik smiled at her, and it was at that moment that she realised something important: she really and truly was no longer in love with him. Or even in lust. Maybe she hadn't been in a long time, but seeing him smile at her, and feeling nothing, and definitely nothing at all like what she'd felt with Darrin, that was a sign.

She suddenly felt stronger. Strong, even. Whatever he was going to say to her, however he was going to try to talk her into giving him her land, her heart, her hope, she wasn't having it.

'We need to talk,' he said.

'You wouldn't be here otherwise.'

'Can we go inside?'

Last week, she would have said yes even though she wouldn't have wanted to. She would have let him talk her into a conversation, and dinner and then he would have attempted to kiss her and she would have turned him down.

He would have left, angry and hurt. But now, she just shook her head. She wasn't sure if it was so easy this time because she knew she wasn't in love with him or because she had a naked man in her bed. Maybe both.

Erik looked surprised for a second, but then buried it behind a different expression.

'It's about the farm.'

'I'm not selling it, Erik. We've had this conversation. Again and again. And again. Just no.' Erik owned more than 400 acres, and ran a hunt club, letting deer hunters from the city come and stalk white tails through the woods. Safe Haven's back woods were almost 100 acres of old apple trees, a deer hunter's heaven. And he wanted them.

'Not about that,' Erik said. His face had an expression she hadn't seen in a long time. Not the persuasive anger she'd grown used to, but something else. 'I saw Ted today, from the bank.'

'And …?' She sounded nonchalant, but her heart had fluttered up into her throat; she could feel the pulse of panic shaking her.

'And he mentioned you were behind in payments. Two months, rolling into a third.'

Kallie's stomach tightened, knots on knots, something that captured her breath and held it tight. 'I told him I was going to be late. I told him I was doing it on my own now. He said it was fine, that he'd give me time.'

The words tumbled out, taking her breath with it. She inhaled, feeling like she was panting, short and shallow breaths.

'Did you do this, Erik? Did you?'

He shook his head beneath his hat, and she believed him. He wanted the land, yes, but she didn't think he was capable of doing that. Not to her.

'Look …' Erik stepped closer to her, and she caught a scent of him, always the way he smelled of pine trees and leather. It was one of the first things she'd lusted after about

166

him. 'I can help you out. I know you're going through a hard time right now, Kal. I could just rent the woods from you for the hunting season. Help you through the rough spot.'

Renting out the woods wasn't something she'd thought of. Erik had always wanted to buy the farm, to turn it into a hunting haven. Renting the woods would let her keep the farm and the animals. At least for a while longer.

But the very idea of having deer hunters traipsing through her woods in orange, the sound of gunshots, the risk of some stupid hunter from NYC shooting at the horses. Everything about it went against all that Safe Haven stood for. Sanctuary. Safety. For her, for the animals. And she knew the unspoken part of the deal too: that he was only offering if she'd agree to go out with him again. Erik never did anything for free.

If she didn't do this, she had no idea how she was going to pay the due mortgage on the land. Nana hadn't left her anything except debt. And when she'd broken up with Erik, he'd stopped helping her support the farm.

'I need ...' she said. He moved even closer until his form was shading her from the sun, until she stood entirely in his shade. 'I need to think about it,' she said finally.

He reached to take her hands, and she was distraught to realise she was going to let him. The calluses he always had slid against her palm, scratching her skin. 'I can help, Kal. I don't have to take it away to make it work.'

She dropped her head, feeling stupid, hot tears in her eyes. Was she so weak? Was it even weak to want something so badly, to want Safe Haven so strongly, that she was willing to give up part of herself? 'I know,' she said. 'I need ... some time. Just some time is all.'

Eric's face changed suddenly, hardening, although he didn't let go of her hand. At the same moment, Kallie heard the front door open, and the quick, welcoming bark of a puppy.

'Hey there!' came Darrin's voice across the lawn. The

words were full of confusion and question, as was Eric's face, and Kallie didn't even have to look behind her to know that not only had Darrin witnessed the whole exchange, but that he was probably standing on her front porch, half-naked, wearing little more than his boxers and a smile.

After Kallie had left, Darrin had sat up to peer through the bedroom window. It wasn't Shar's truck; it was a big black four-by-four. The man in it was big too, wide as a doorway, and nearly as tall. Kallie was striding toward him, clearly unhappy to see him there. Even in her anger, the curls of her hair shone and her ass wiggled just as cute when she was pissed as when she was happy. He would have to make a mental note of that.

They didn't look like they were having a happy conversation. From Kallie's stance to the way she kept her arms crossed over her chest, he figured she was not happy to see the man who'd just landed in her driveway. In fact, he thought she'd welcomed him much the same way when he'd arrived with motorcycle and puppy in tow.

He couldn't hear what the two were saying, though, and he was torn between going out there and staying here. On one hand, he thought she might want help, on the other, he thought she seemed pretty capable of handling things on her own.

Then the man touched Kallie.

Darrin told himself he wasn't a jealous person. He told himself he didn't have any right to this wonderful, gorgeous woman who'd so quickly managed to get into his heart and his pants. He told himself that he'd just met her. He knew almost nothing about her, except that every time she smiled or dipped her head or opened her mouth, he wanted to kiss her. And more than that, he wanted to fuck her, to feel her shudder beneath him and above him, to hear her say his name in that sweet, soft voice of hers.

He told this to himself, and to Gauntlet, as the two

watched the exchange through Kallie's bedroom window. Gauntlet just whined and wagged his tail, as if telling Darrin that everything he was saying was completely true.

But when the man had reached out to touch Kallie's hand and Kallie had bent her head as if the very touch had broken her, Darrin had pulled on his pants and headed toward the front door, calling Gauntlet after him.

Then he'd felt stupid, standing there half-dressed, while the guy had tried to stare him down. Kallie hadn't looked his way, hadn't even acknowledged his hello or his wave, and that made things even worse. He wished he'd stayed inside. He wished he'd dropped the puppy off at the pound, instead of coming here. Where so far he'd got bit, had squealed in pain, and managed to embarrass himself at least twice more.

'Howdy,' the man said, giving him a slow half-nod under his cowboy hat. He wore dark jeans, a pair of work gloves tucked in the back pocket, his checked shirt rolled up to the elbows. He looked real, like a man Darrin might have liked in another place, in another time. But right now, he wasn't sure of anything.

'Be seeing you,' the man said to Kallie as he pulled himself into the truck. 'Think about it. Season opens in just a couple weeks. Enough time for you to make your pay.'

The man got into his truck, lifting one finger off the steering wheel, either in a flip-off or a wave, and then pulled out and down the long driveway. The horses didn't even lift their heads at the sound.

Kallie was still standing in the driveway where the man had left her. She looked deflated, smaller, like all the air had gone out of her somewhere between the house and here. Darrin wanted to put his lips to her mouth, to blow her back into life, into joy.

'Kallie?' he asked.

She flapped her hand at him, a half-gesture of go-away, plus something else he didn't understand. Even with her head down, her hair falling over her face, he could see she was crying, the tear trails glossing her cheeks.

'What happened?' he asked. This time she did look up, her eyes narrow, the laugh-lines that he'd traced earlier completely disappearing. He was suddenly sure she was going to be angry, or flippant, that she was going to say, 'Nothing,' in that pissed off tone that meant everything, that meant she was going to stalk off. It was one of the things he'd hated the most about the models he worked with; their inability to have an honest conversation when things were hard. In fact, he became so sure she would respond like that, that he could feel the weight in his chest already, the loss of her.

Finally, she released a long slow breath and then spoke. 'It's a long story. And complicated.'

He felt himself recoil from the words as though they were so unexpected he could feel them sinking into his skin. He had no idea how to react to that, but he still felt this wonderful sense of relief, of her ability to truly talk about things.

Gauntlet pounced between them, stalking a bug between their feet. Darrin watched the puppy for a second, unsure how much to push her. He bent down and scooped the puppy up, then held him out to Kallie. She took him instantly, curled her arms around the ball of fur and then lifted him up to kiss his puppy nose.

'Careful,' Darrin teased, wanting nothing more than to see her smile. 'You'll make me jealous.'

Her smile, when it came, was quick and more full of sadness than he would have liked.

'Do you want to talk about it?' he asked finally. 'Yes,' she said, surprising him again. 'But not quite yet. Could I have a little time?'

He nodded, suddenly glad he didn't have to speak. Something had hit him in the throat, an emotion or a sense of hope, something so big that he wasn't sure he could have got words out around it. He hadn't felt that in a long, long time and he suddenly realised that he was in far more trouble than a horse bite, a stray puppy and a bit of embarrassment.

Chapter Five

SHE SHOULD HAVE RIDDEN Toddy – he needed the practice more than the others, but her head wasn't on straight and it wouldn't be fair to ask him to behave when she couldn't give him the attention he needed. So she grabbed a bridle and hunted down Memphis, a middle-aged mare that had been her first rescue. Memphis rarely went faster than a slow canter, but she didn't need a saddle and she wasn't likely to reach around and bite Kallie in the knee while her mind was elsewhere.

They headed out along the back pasture and then into the woods, following the wide truck trails at first and then threaded off into the smaller footpaths and deer tracks. Memphis' wide, warm back swayed beneath Kallie, their pace something barely above a meander. When Kallie had been young, her nana had owned all this land. It had been a horse farm then, for boarding and riding. Kallie had adored the horses, the barn, her nana's cookie-smelling house. But the woods had scared her. Dark and closed-in, she'd felt like she was being watched or pursued.

As an adult, she'd lost much of her fear, but still felt like the woods carried something magical and inexplicable, something that was best treated with respect and not disturbed. What Erik wanted to do – bring in hunters, men with their big voices and big guns to sit in shelters and shoot deer for sport – it wasn't something that felt right to Kallie. And yet, she knew she was behind on her payments. When she and Erik had been a couple, he'd mostly supported her through those early months of starting Safe Haven. The farm brought in a little when she sold a recouped animal or did training or boarding on the side, but never enough to sustain it. She was grateful to Erik, but when she'd realised they weren't working as a couple any more, when he'd started using the money as a power thing over her, she'd ended it. And then she'd had to go to Ted at the bank and ask for an extension. It hurt in all kinds of ways, mostly her heart and her pride, but what hurt worse was realising she couldn't see any good way out of the dilemma. If she took Erik up on his offer, she'd be able to save the farm, but at a cost. And he'd expect her to come back to him; she'd seen in it his eyes, in the way he'd touched her hand. In the way she'd let him.

And then there was Darrin. Darrin of the blue eyes and ice-melting smile. Darrin of the stray puppies and savoury kisses. Darrin, who'd asked for her to kiss him, who'd arched beneath the very touch of her hands as though he hadn't probably touched or fucked in far too long. Darrin who had made her wet with want a hundred times today already.

Darrin who had asked her if she'd wanted to talk, and when she'd asked for time, he'd said OK, just like that. No guilt, no fear, no pressure. Anyone else who'd asked, she would have said she was fine. She'd even expected to say, 'No, I'd rather not talk about it.' But what had come out was something else, as though she was considering opening up her entire life's story to some near-stranger. What was it about this guy that made her want to just invite him in?

Maybe it was the way he seemed to know what she needed. How he'd given her the puppy first, something to hold on to, and then had been a quiet presence while she'd steadied herself. She didn't think it was easy for him, the staying quiet for as long as he did. She wanted to say how she appreciated that, but the words were all tangled up somewhere between her chest and the puppy, who'd been busy attempting to lick her mouth.

Erik. Darrin. Gauntlet. The farm. Herself. At least three

of those needed saving. And she had no idea how to do any of it.

As they ambled along, Memphis snorting occasionally at the wayward rabbit or squirrel that sprinted away from their movement, Kallie put a plan together. In order to save the farm, she'd say yes to Erik. She had to. It meant that much to her.

But in the meantime, she was going to go back home and continue what she'd started with the incredibly hot, incredibly sweet man in her bed. If he even was still in her bed.

Kallie had a mental picture of Darrin as she'd left him hours before, mostly naked, the lean muscles of his chest and biceps. The way he'd moaned lightly the first time she'd touched his cock, how it had jumped lightly beneath her fingers. The sweet taste of his mouth. How much she'd been anticipating tasting him, tonguing his length.

What the hell was she doing out here? If she had demons that needed handling out among the trees, they could certainly wait.

Nudging Memphis into a soft canter, she urged the mare quickly back toward home. They broke from the trees at a slow run, slipping across the pasture just in time to catch the first strands of sunset over the pines. *A couple of days,* Shar had said. Kallie could do a lot in a couple of days, she realised. Then Darrin would be gone, Gauntlet would be gone and she could go back to Erik. She could save them both and Safe Haven. She just couldn't figure out how to save herself.

By the time Kallie had Memphis cooled down and thing cleared up around the barn, it was nearly full dark, only a few streaks of grey across the lower sky. She'd checked the driveway before starting the chores, just to see if the thing with Erik had scared Darrin away. Darrin's motorcycle was still there, shining in the falling light. It made her feel both giddy and nervous, but mostly it left her filled with a kind of hot, delighted desire. She would be throwing hay and the scent of him would hit her, or she'd hear the way he'd asked her to come and kiss him, and she would be filled with a longing that shuddered through her and left her gasping. And laughing a little too – she hadn't even managed to have sex with the man, and here she was, breathless at the very thought.

She was standing in Toddy's stall, crooning to him, a carrot on her flat palm, waiting to see if he'd come and take it, when she realised what she was doing out here. All she'd wanted to do was come home and fuck the man, but now she was here she hadn't even gone in to try and find him. She was, instead, sing-songing to a big dumb scared horse about how big dumb and scared he was.

You chicken, she chided herself. You're afraid to find out if the sex is any good. And you dare call Toddy a big baby.

It was true. Darrin was the perfect play toy, here and then gone, sexy and sweet and clearly as in lust with her as she was with him. And beautiful. Those eyes that had flipped her right-side up and upside down again with barely a glance.

She tossed the carrot into Toddy's feed bin with a half-hearted apology, and nearly ran out the stall door, chiding herself for being such a fool.

Kallie tore into the house, the front door slamming behind her, only to realise that the house was dark and nothing was moving inside. The quiet tick-tick of the wind up alarm was louder than it should have been, and she wasn't surprised to look at the dog pillow and realise that Gauntlet wasn't sleeping on it.

The bedroom had a light on and she went that way, stopping outside the door at the sight of both Darrin and the dog, curled together, sound asleep. He was still half-dressed, shirtless, Gauntlet tucked against his chest, one puppy paw thrown over Darrin's arm. Darrin's hair was damp, which made it darker and curlier, and it smelled like her shampoo.

175

She stood looking down at them, watching the rise and fall of puppy belly, the soft movement of Darrin's eyes behind his lids. Even with those blue eyes hidden, even sound asleep, there was something dynamic about him, something that called to her. She wanted to run her bare hands over his skin, to feel the breath that he drew, to slip her fingers into his jeans and feel the dark hair that rested there, coiled and wiry.

His breathing changed slightly, so that she wondered if he was awake or just shifting in his sleep, when he said, 'I can feel you.'

'I'm not touching you,' she said.

'I feel you staring.'

'Would you like to feel me doing other things?'

One eye opened, blue as a gem. 'Yes.'

'Like what?'

The other eye opened, and his voice, already husked with sleep and dream, dropped to a whisper. 'Can we get rid of the puppy before I tell you? I don't want to corrupt him.'

Not bothering to reply, she scooped the drowsing puppy up and cradled him, then deposited him on the pillow with the ticking clock. He wriggled, whining, and she stood over him, holding her breath, afraid to move lest she wake him. If she had one more interruption today – from an ex, from herself, from a puppy – without getting to have sex, she thought she might explode.

Chapter Six

THANKFULLY, GAUNTLET SETTLED BACK in, although she didn't know how much free time she had before he woke, and she practically ran back to the bedroom.

Darrin was fully awake now, lying on the bed, one hand stroking his cock through the fabric of his jeans, his grin somewhere between sheepish and excited.

'I couldn't wait,' he said.

'I was only gone for two minutes,' she said, but there was something in his desire, his confession – she'd never known anyone so upfront about his wants – that made her instantly wet, a tumbling river of want that swept through her.

'And hours before that ...' He stretched the word out like a little kid who'd been waiting for a treat, a half-believable pout forming on his face at the end of it.

'Well, then,' she said. 'Who am I to stop you? By all means, please continue.'

'But ...' That pout. On most guys, it would look stupid or needy. On him, it was just so fucking adorable, and somehow – she had no idea how – hot. 'You're here now. And I have been on the road for ...' His expression was thoughtful, and she got the impression that if she wasn't in the room, he would have been counting on his fingers. '... many weeks. Which means I am very, very, very tired of being left to my own devices by now.'

On the road that long. She realised that although she knew why he was travelling, she didn't really know who he was, or what he was hoping for, or where he'd come from. Most of the men she'd slept with had grown up here, or moved here years ago, she knew their whole lives, their dating history, their futures. This man, enigma wrapped in a riddle, a phrase she'd always loved, but had never gotten to use *about* someone before.

She stood a long moment, her arms crossed over her shoulders, taking the sight of him in yet again. Wide shoulders, muscled. The smooth chest, with just enough hair that made her want to snuggle up against it. The lean hips, the curve of his cock beneath the curve of his fingers and fabric.

'Oh, please,' he said. 'You're a horrible tease. And by horrible, I mean not a very good one. Come and kiss me again. I've waited very patiently, for a very long time, for someone like you to kiss me again.'

There was something buried there, in his words, something beyond lust, but she didn't let herself hear it. Instead, she shook it away with a joke.

'Someone like me?'

'Someone exactly like you.'

She went to him, his hand taking hers to pull her onto the bed, on top of him, and then they were kissing again. His tongue opened her lips, insistent, searching, his body pushing upward to meet hers, the length of his cock pressing into the hollow between her thighs.

'Wait,' he said, and he pushed her up by the shoulders until he could look into her eyes. In the near-dark, they were a purpled grey, and she couldn't stop looking at them, even as some part of her registered that he was pushing her away. 'I need to know something ...'

Her gut tightened and she could feel her face doing that thing that it did, also tightening, a frown probably, a look of fear too. She swallowed it away the best she could. Whatever he asked, she would tell him the truth. 'OK.'

'If another truck comes up the drive, are you going to jump out of bed again, leaving me naked and hard and then run away for hours? Because I'm OK with a little kinky power-play, but that's not really ...'

'Shut up,' she said, and wriggled out of his grip until she could kiss him again, taking charge this time, opening his mouth with the press of her lips and tongue, urging him harder against her, nipping at his lips when they broke apart. He pressed his mouth, soft, open so she could feel his breath, against the crook of her neck, down to her shoulder, up to her ear. She could hear her own breath, quick exhales full of want.

When he tugged her jeans open, she felt it all the way through her body, an electric pulse of arousal. It took only a single movement – his hand slipping inside her jeans, turning to circle a single finger against her clit – and she was lost, the edges of her body no longer defined by anything except for the touch of his skin, the press of his mouth to hers.

'Off, off, off,' he said, the impatient one this time, tugging at her clothes just as she was at his, until they were both fully naked, feeling her nipples tighten against his chest, the length of his cock bobbing against her thigh as she shifted.

She took his cock in her fingers, loving the way its heft filled her palm, the pale length of it, the curved head that already shone with a bit of moisture.

He laughed as she curved her fist around it.

'What?' she asked.

'I guess that's the end of the kissing?'

'No,' she said, and she leaned down and put her lips against the curved head, inhaling just enough to taste the heated want of him. He twitched against her mouth, moaning low in the back of his throat. Parting her lips, she sucked him, feeling the slide of his smooth, clean skin, the way his erection hardened and grew as he sunk into her. She pulled away for a moment, looking up at him, loving the heated, lightly glazed expression on his face. 'This is considered kissing, right?'

Hearing him moan, she couldn't resist putting a hand between her thighs as she began to suck him, surprised at how wet she already was, how easily she parted for the press of her fingers.

'Let me,' he said, pushing her hand away, his own fingertips searching out the wettest parts of her, beginning with soft, slow strokes that made her own movements falter, her quiet gasps rising despite the way he filled her mouth, took her breath away.

His touch was exploratory, not hesitant, but waiting for her responses before he moved on, allowing her quiet moans to guide him. She tried to focus on her own movements, the push and pull of her mouth along his cock, slick and hard with want, the way his skin felt against the draw of her tongue, but she found herself unable to focus as his touch deepened against the point of her clit, circling it with ever-tighter curls.

She gave up sucking him actively, and let his length rest on her tongue, keeping him deep inside. He lowered his mouth to her nipple, brushing his tongue along it, the same inquisitive touch he'd used elsewhere, and then opening his lips and taking the sensitive point lightly between his teeth.

Tiny sparks of impatient want cascaded through her. If he kept that up, she thought she might come, but she didn't want to. Not yet, not without feeling him enter her first. She gave him another long, slow suck, tasting the sweetly salted want at the very head, and then said, 'I don't think I can wait any more.'

'Well, that's not good enough.' His fingers worked against her skin, small pinches that made her ache and arch.

'I ... can't wait any more ... please.'

'Better.' He nipped the corner of her nipple, sending more sparks along her, then grinned up at her. 'Then I think now would be a great time to go off for a while and leave you here, naked and panting.'

'Jerk,' she said. The teasing made her hotter, not cooler,

her insides flowing with a liquid want.

'You did it first.' He pulled her toward him, laying the length of his body over her own, slipping the very tip of his cock against her wetness. She ached for him to be all the way inside her, and yet she savoured the sensation of the tease, like slowly unwrapping a gift.

'You left me here,' he said, each word punctuated with another too-soft stroke of his tip against her. 'Naked, hard, dreaming about having your mouth against mine, seeing you naked for the first time, doing this ...'

He dropped his mouth to her breasts, first one then the other, sucking them hard and deep, her hips bucking up in a tangled response that started at her nipples and worked its way down to the very spot where his cock met her skin.

'I'd like to fuck you,' he said. That question, not a question she was beginning to adore.

'I'd like you to fuck me, too,' she said.

'But ...'

'There's a but?'

'There's a wonderful butt,' he said, grinning. 'But there's also the fact that I was not prepared to fall into someone's arms. Or into their body, either.'

She came back into her body for a moment, wishing that she hadn't. 'Is this a big emotional talk? Because if so, I'd really prefer to have it post-sex.'

'This is the "I've never been a very good Boy Scout" talk.'

It took her a second to get it.

'Oh,' she said. 'Condoms. Top drawer.'

He found one and tried to put it on, getting it backwards, rolling his eyes. 'They should make these things with "This Side Up" signs.'

She took the rubber from him and flipped it, laughing. 'Let me.' Condoms weren't the sexiest things to fuck with, but she actually liked this part, pushing the material down over a long hard cock, watching his erection become encased in see-through, the way his cock twitched in her hand as she unrolled it over him. It was a beautiful thing between her hands, and touching it like this made her want him inside her even more.

Clearly, he felt the same way, because he teased her with his fingers for only a moment longer before he pushed her down gently to kneel between her thighs. He put his hands under her ass and lifted her up. He entered her with a sharp push that took her breath away, and fitted into her with a sensation that would have been too much if not for how wet she was. He started slow, pulling back with a heated groan that tugged a ragged sound of pleasure from her, returning to fill her until he was buried deep within her, his hips melding to her own.

He kissed her as he fucked her. It started soft and slow, controlled, and then moved into something else entirely, their mouths connecting hard and fast on each stroke, a clash of teeth and lips that would have hurt in any other circumstance, but in this case just added to the pleasure, to the urgent need that Kallie had to feel him fill her again and again.

He pulled away, eliciting a moan from Kallie. 'What?'

'Flip, please.' It was a request, but one that he was fulfilling even as he spoke, turning her over and lifting her from the bed. 'So I can touch you while I fuck you,' he said, as though he were answering a question she hadn't asked. 'And look at your ass too, of course.'

She was about to make a snide remark, but his arm slid around her, his fingers finding her clit again, remembering the things she'd responded to earlier, touching her at just the right speed, keeping time to his strokes. And when she opened her mouth to say something, only a keened moan came out, a quiet release of his name even as her body released around him, the strength of her orgasm surprising her into sharp shudders and soft whimpers.

'Kallie,' he whispered, biting lightly at the edge of her

ear, and she might have come again, just from that, she wasn't sure, because he was releasing into her, long slow strokes and the sound of her name again and again, and she couldn't tell any more what was her body and what was his.

Chapter Seven

'CAN WE TALK ABOUT what happened earlier?' he asked after, stroking Kallie's hair, wishing he could photograph the way the colours intermingled, the way a single curl fell across her cheekbone. He didn't want to ruin the moment with serious questions, but he knew two things about himself: one, his curiosity was going to get the best of him and two, he was falling for this girl and falling hard, and he needed to know what, exactly, was waiting for him at the bottom of that fall.

Kallie snuggled up against him, fitting perfectly against his body, her head resting on his shoulder. When she opened her eyes, he was shocked as he always was, at the dark beauty of her gaze, how it was possible to see her intelligence and warmth in the colours alone.

She took a long time before she answered, and he could see she was struggling with her word choice. 'Safe Haven has been my dream since I was little. It's something that my nana and I used to talk about. This was her land, her house, her barns. When she died a few years ago, she left it all to me so that I could start Safe Haven.'

She closed her eyes and in that single gesture, he saw so much about her. He could picture her for a moment as a young girl, in love with her grandmother, in love with helping animals, building a dream even at that age. He swallowed down his first instinct, which was to say something helpful but stupid, and just held her tighter while she talked.

'She thought she was giving me a gift, and she was,

really. But the land wasn't totally paid for – I think she thought it was – but when they did the legal stuff, they realised she still owed a lot. Well, that I owed a lot.'

'When was that?' he asked. Her grief, while palpable in her big eyes, didn't seem fresh, but it was hard to tell. Everyone carried that differently.

'Almost a year.'

'And you've kept the farm going until now?' Her gazed shifted away and she found something on the blanket to pick at while she talked.

'Sort of. No, not really. I was seeing someone who was helping me. Financially at least. Emotionally, not so much.'

'The man with the really big truck?'

She laughed. 'You say truck like most people say penis. But yes. Him.'

'And?'

'And it wasn't working and we ended it and now ...' she swallowed loud enough for him to hear it. He put his hand over hers, forced her fingers to stop picking at the invisible blanket lint. 'Well, he's offered me a way to keep the farm going. I have to take it.'

'A money offer.'

'Yes,' she said. 'And.'

The "and" was a complete sentence in itself somehow. At least, he thought he knew everything that it entailed. Darrin wanted to prompt her for more, but he didn't want to push her. After all, what could he offer her? He had money, but that felt presumptuous. A trip out of town on his motorcycle? A new puppy? She clearly loved the land and the farm. He couldn't take her away from it. And he couldn't stay. He had a job that was waiting for him at the end of his travels. A job on the opposite coast.

Not to mention, what was he even thinking? He'd known her for ... he realised he had to count back ... he felt like he'd known her forever, but in truth, it was no time at all. Not even a day. Certainly not enough to feel the way he was feeling. She was a stranger, he reminded himself, and yet he felt like he knew her better than people he'd known for years, for a decade even.

Instead of pushing her, he did the only thing he could think of that might help: he buried his hands softly in her curls and pulled her against him, let her bury her face in his chest, and he held her so tight he thought she might not be able to breathe OK. It wasn't until he felt her sobbing against him quietly, the crying shaking her whole body, that he realised she could definitely breathe, but she was definitely not OK.

He held her until she fell asleep, until her breathing quieted to nothing. And then he lay next to her and watched her, the beauty of her in this rare moment of quiet stillness, how she was always moving except for now, when her body curled into a soft, silent curve against him. As always, his fingers itched for his camera, but he resisted, worrying he'd wake her, and instead he just soaked it in. He didn't move until he heard Gauntlet pad into the bedroom, his soft whines clear requests for sharing the bed. Darrin rolled over and pulled the puppy up, settling his warm form between the two of them.

Gauntlet licked Kallie's sleeping face, making Darrin laugh.

'I agree, Gaunt. She's totally lickable.'

She was more than lickable. She was everything he'd ever wanted in a woman. And she was completely unattainable.

It was dawn, past dawn, and Kallie wanted nothing more than to stay snuggled against the warm sleeping man who shared her bed. But that was the truth of a farm, any farm, but especially of a rescue farm: There were not enough hours in the day and staying in bed meant a hundred things that didn't get done. And layered into that, a sense of panic and sorrow that she didn't know how much longer Safe

186

Haven would be fully hers. That thought alone, was enough to pull her fully awake and out of bed.

Still, she couldn't resist stealing a kiss from Darrin as he lay on his back, his breathing deep and regular, the sound turning into a soft murmur as her lips touched his. She had come to love his smell lately, and she leaned in to draw her nose along the curve of his neck, inhaling. It was only a second later that she realised why he smelled so good to her; he'd been here a couple of days already and he'd taken on the scent of the farm, of sweet hay and clean animals and cold water. He'd begun to smell like home.

Kallie pushed herself from bed, trying not to wake him, unnerved at the realisation. He was supposed to be, just for now. Just until he was better and gone, just until she could bear to do what needed to happen next with Erik. But the longer he stayed, the more she realised that she didn't want anything to do with Eric's proposal. It was depressing, being stuck. And scary. Darrin was a fun diversion, but that's all he was. All he could be.

'Where you going?' he asked, his voice thick with sleep and want. She stopped at the door, unable to resist looking back over her shoulder. He was snuggled beneath the blankets, only his face peeking out. Those bright blue eyes, still half-asleep but somehow shimmering with want. For her. At her.

'Chores,' she said, but already she was rationalising things in her head. If she crawled back in bed with him for just another couple of minutes, thcy could ...

'Come and fuck me first?' he asked, one hand sneaking out of the blankets and beckoning at her.

'Hmm ...' she said. 'I'll make you a deal.'

He squinted at her, eyes narrowing slightly, but his smile growing. 'I like deals ... especially ones that involve me inside you.'

'I'll come back to bed if you'll help me with chores later.'

'OK,' he said, too quickly.

'You don't even know what that means, do you?'

'It means I get to entice you back into bed and ravage your delicious body for a little while, right?'

'I'm just going to say yes,' she said. 'We can work out the details later.' She slid back beneath the covers, snuggling up to his body, laughing when she felt his cock nudge her thigh. 'Ooh,' she said, rolling him over so that she could sit on his hips, nestling the length of his cock between her thighs. She curled her hips against him, loving the quiet, sleepy breaths that issued from him.

Lifting herself up, she stroked his length, then lowered herself down slowly, letting it fill her as his hips lifted upward to meet her, and push into her. Darrin's hands took hold of her hips, tight, his nails digging in lightly as he stroked her above him. His eyes were closed, his mouth half-open as he groaned in time to their movements, shuddering lightly beneath her. He was so beautiful, the width of his shoulders, the jaw that tightened each time he pushed up full into her.

'Open your eyes,' she whispered, her own voice half-lost in lust and need and pleasure.

He did as she asked, looking up at her, the blue of his gaze heated and coiled. 'Kallie,' he whispered, harsh and needing, the very sound of her name becoming a thing that carried his pleasure.

'Please,' she said, and he reached out to touch her, one hand cupping her breast, his thumb rubbing soft circles over the sensitive peak of her nipple, the other sliding between them, the very tip of his finger lightly stroking her clit.

'Kallie,' he said again. 'Come for me ...'

And she couldn't help it, couldn't have stopped herself even if she wanted to, the way he filled her and touched her and circled her and most of all, saw her. She called his name, hard and sudden, as the pleasure overtook her. He drove up into her, hard and fast through her orgasm, until he was coming himself, calling out her name again and again into the morning light.

Chapter Eight

IT ONLY TOOK A few more days before Darrin felt stronger on his feet. Slow, but able to keep up with the bumbling puppy at least. And he'd been helping Kallie around the farm, which was helping, in some odd way that he couldn't articulate. It felt good to be doing work that made his muscles sore, even if he didn't always know exactly what he was doing.

Kallie had taken off early for something farmish – he wasn't sure he understood all that she did to keep the place afloat, but he did understand that it was a lot – and so he wandered around the house, touching things here and there, picking up books, putting them down. He didn't feel restless, exactly, but more as though there was something he should be doing, something that kept slipping through his fingers.

A glance outside the window brought it all home to him. Kallie had returned while he'd been pottering, and now she stood in the field, surrounded by the horses she'd rescued. The wind was high, and they pranced around her, full of energy. At some unknown thing, they gathered as a group and took off running, tails and manes whipping into waves. They reminded him of Kallie when she rode or even just moved through the world, wild in a tameable way. It was something that they always aimed for with models, but there it was something they'd had to create. Here, it was real. Kallie was real.

He hadn't touched his camera in three weeks, and he fumbled for it now, pulling it from his travel bag in the living room.

'Come on, pup.' Gauntlet, always ready go to outside, took little urging before he was waiting at the door, tail thumping against Darrin's leg.

Outside, the wind had picked up, sending leaves cascading around them as they made their way to the pasture. There was so much to photograph here. He'd wanted to shoot Kallie, of course, since the moment he'd seen her coming out of the barn. And every time he'd seen her since then, whether she was working or sleeping or, especially, when she was fucking, grinning at him wickedly over her shoulder, or taking him into her mouth, or even just that moment when orgasm rolled over her, her mouth open, eyes half-closed, their hue darkening in pleasure.

But there was all of this too. The horses playing at being wild in the wind. Kallie in the centre, the thing they left and returned to in a way that reminded him of children playing, coming back to check that all was well. He didn't think she'd seen him; her back was mostly to him, the curve of her ass beneath her winter coat, the length of her hair mimicking the horses'.

He anchored himself carefully against the wooden fence and started shooting. Everything caught his attention. The things that moved, the things that didn't. But most of all, what filled his lens was Kallie. Her laugh as one of the horses came up to her and head-butted her almost hard enough to knock her over. That moment when she caught sight of him, and realised that he'd been shooting her, and she stuck her tongue out at him from across the field. Even the way she strode toward him, her stride fake-angry, the half-grin on her face giving her away. He was suddenly glad he'd shot these; it was at least something he could take back home with him, a reminder that there was a place where things – and people – were real.

'What, pray tell, are you doing out here?' she asked. 'It's cold.'

He let the camera fall against his chest, suddenly realising how long he'd been out here. His fingers were stiff from the wind. 'Would it be too woo-woo to say I'm finding myself? Or maybe my passion?'

She leaned against him, bringing the smell of cold apples with her, kissing his chin lightly. 'If this is your passion, I'd say it's rather frigid.'

'*One* of my passions,' he said, surprising himself even as he said it, because it was true. Kallie was becoming a passion. Or maybe igniting his passion. Or maybe a little of both.

'Mmm,' she said. 'Maybe it's time to explore one of your non-freezing passions then.'

He curved his hands around her ass and pulled her as close as he could around the bulk of the camera. 'Like hot chocolate with tiny marshmallows?'

Her laugh, that surprised delight that bubbled from her. That was something he couldn't capture with his camera. No matter how much he wanted to. So many things he was going to have to leave behind. The sound of her, the smell, the feel of her around his fingers, inside his mouth.

He would take everything he could get for now. 'Sounds perfect,' he said, but even he could hear the hollow sound of his words.

Kallie took his hand and led him toward the house, the puppy bounding along behind them.

Inside, it was too hot against his cold skin, but Kallie was cold too, and he undressed her as fast as he could with half-frozen fingers.

'Gah, no touching!' she squealed when he finally got down through her layers to reveal her pale skin.

'But how can I fuck you if I can't touch you?' he asked. 'And I so very much want to fuck you.' It was true. She was standing before him, covered in goose bumps, her arms crossed just under the curves of her breasts, her nipples pink and pointed.

192

'I suppose you'll have to find a way,' she said.

He leaned down and curled his tongue about one nipple, relishing its firmness, relishing even more her quiet sighs of pleasure. She put her hands in his hair, holding him there lightly, her head falling back as she groaned, quiet and guttural. 'I love kissing you, and sucking you,' he said, taking a quiet breath before he bent his head to mouth her other nipple, tasting her skin, like apples and honey on his tongue. 'And fucking you ...' The other nipple. 'And when you suck me ...' Back to the second one with a loud suckle, just a bit of his teeth across her sensitive point. Her low moan and the way her fingers tightened in his hair made his cock pulse and strain against his jeans. How was it possible to want her so fiercely, so often? He kept thinking that he would fuck away his need, that his desire for her would lessen, but it kept growing and growing.

'Fuck, Darrin,' she groaned, and that was that desire again, rising up inside him, making him growl low in his throat as he leaned up to kiss her mouth, letting his tongue meet hers, sucking her lip in between her teeth.

'Please,' she said. 'Pleasepleaseplease.' Her words running together, her breath and speech against his mouth, her cool hands reaching down to open his jeans, to take his cock in her hands, to go down on her knees, naked before him, sinking his length slowly into the heat of her mouth. Now it was his turn to sigh and moan, to growl low as want became pleasure and pleasure became want and the two intermingled until he couldn't breathe, until he could barely stand, even his good leg shaking, threatening to give way.

'Wait,' he said. 'Kallie, wait ... I want to ...' So many things he wanted to do, but as he looked down at her, the dancing light in her eyes as she continued to stroke him with her mouth, the way her cool hand tightened around the base of his cock, lightly joining in the rhythm, he knew she wasn't going to let him do any of them. At least not yet.

So he gave in to the pleasure she was giving him instead,

let it build inside him.

Until she pulled away, grinning up at him and licking her lips. He tried not to fall over at the unexpected release of her mouth.

'Hot chocolate time!' she yelled, getting up and running toward the kitchen. He'd never seen her run so fast, the white curves of her ass bouncing deliciously as she ran.

'Tease!' he yelled.

'Yes!' she yelled back.

'Just wait until I catch you,' he said. He was trying to figure out how to follow her with an erection, unbuttoned jeans and an ache in his calf.

'Oh, trust me,' she said. 'I am so waiting ...'

When he finally got to the kitchen, she was sitting on the counter, her legs spread and hanging over the edge. 'That doesn't look like hot chocolate,' he said.

'Just as tasty.' She grinned at him, which nearly made him laugh. Drawing close to her, ignoring the pain in his leg, he bent his head to taste her, to savour in the sweet scent of her, in the way her clit grew tight and wet beneath the brush of his tongue. He could, he thought, do this forever. If only he could figure out how.

Chapter Nine

BY THE TIME DAWN broke the next morning, bright and cold, Kallie had fed all the animals and was reworking her way through them, giving special attention where it was needed. Gauntlet had made it clear he was coming with her and so she'd brought him along with her on the tongue-promise that he wouldn't chase the ducklings or any of the other animals. So far, he'd made good on the promise, occupying himself by attacking the shifting bits of straw or by chewing on the rope toy she'd found earlier.

She was just finishing up grooming the long-haired rabbits when she heard someone clear their throat.

'Morning,' Darrin said. He was leaning against the barn door jamb, dressed in a pair of jeans that looked like they'd come out of his backpack pre-pressed and a white button-up shirt. It was the stupidest thing to wear to a barn that Kallie had ever seen – he'd be dirty and rumpled in no time flat – but it was also so sexy that it made her heart beat as quickly as the rabbit's in her lap. The sun was coming up behind him, highlighting his dark curls and his wide shoulders beneath the white shirt. She remembered last night, the way he'd slipped into the shower after her, gone down on his knees beneath the spray of water, tongue and fingers worked her into an orgasm that had left her shaken and unsteady. Her body gave a silent moan of want, which she desperately tried to ignore.

'Morning,' she said. 'How's the bite?'

'Actually, it feels pretty good. I thought I might try getting back on the bike today, see how it feels.' The revelation made her heart slow back down, ponderous thumps that thudded against her breastbone. You're supposed to be happy he's leaving, she thought. That's the plan, right?

She slid the rabbit back into his cage. He thumped his hind legs once, a noise loud enough to pull Gauntlet's head up, both ears pricked. Kallie refused to voice how cute he was. How cute they both were. How at-home they looked wherever they were in Safe Haven. The barn, the house, her bed ...

Well, if he was going, then she was going to take advantage of him before he was gone. Wasn't that part of her plan too?

She slipped forward until she nearly reached Darrin, the dawning light warm on her face after the coolness of the barn. She wanted nothing more than to kiss him again, to feel the insistent press of his lips to hers. Leaning in, she told herself that one more time wouldn't mean anything. It was just a kiss. A sexy kiss that usually left her breathless and wanting.

Just as her lips touched his, he pulled back suddenly. She barely caught herself as she pitched forward, her cheeks burning with sudden embarrassment and confusion.

'Sorry,' she mumbled, turning away, her face already burning. Maybe now that he was feeling better, he was already ready to leave. She'd just assumed he wouldn't go so fast ...

'No,' he said quickly as he took hold of her arm. 'It's just the uh ...' He fumbled, pointed at her shirt.

Kallie looked down and realised she was covered in rabbit hair. Big fluffy tufts of orange-white hair hung from every fold of her shirt. 'Oh, shit,' she said.

'This is the only clean shirt I have left,' he said. 'It's not that I don't want to kiss you – because I do – it's just that you look like you're growing yellow hair.'

'I can fix that,' she said. She grabbed her T-shirt at the

hem and pulled it up over her head, then let it fall to the ground next to her. 'Better?' she asked.

'Well, there is that other odd fur in the way ...'

'Odd ... what?'

He ran his fingers over the lace at the top of her bra, sending shivers through her. 'This stuff. In the way. Bad joke. It's not fur. Clearly.'

'I can fix that too,' she said, reaching behind her to unsnap her bra. In the cold air and the proximity of him, her nipples tightening into sharp points.

The very act of him reaching out to touch one made her gasp.

'What about your pants?' he asked.

'Oh, I'm going to let you fix that,' she said.

'Really?'

'Yes,' she said. She leaned in and kissed him, teasing his tongue with her own. This morning, he tasted of coffee and cream and sweetness. She wanted to drink him up.

'Won't someone see?' he asked, but the question didn't stop his hips from meeting hers, the already stiffening length of his cock nudging her through the fabric.

'The horses couldn't care less,' she said. 'And clearly Gauntlet doesn't.'

'I meant, like, out there ...' He was nipping at the side of her neck, exploratory bites that made her crazy with want.

'We'll hear the doorbell.'

The quizzical look on his face was almost enough to make her laugh. 'Later,' she said by way of explanation. 'For now, how about you just come with me, Mr fuzzy butt?'

'I'm not the one who's fuzzy!'

'Have you seen your butt lately?'

His face scrunched up in the most amusing way when he was thinking. It made her want to run her fingertips over the little wrinkles that lined either side of his nose.

She took his hand and led him to the wooden ladder that

ran up the middle of the barn. 'Up,' she said.

'The hay loft?' he asked, giving her a raised brow. 'How gauche.'

'I'm all about the clichés,' she said.

'What about Gauntlet?'

'He's hardly looking needy at the moment.' They both looked at the puppy, who had fallen asleep on a pile of straw, his big full puppy belly rising and falling in time to his little snores.

She moved behind Darrin and put her hands on his denim-covered ass, giving him a soft push. 'Up?'

'I'm scared of heights,' he said, but it wasn't believable, especially since he was already taking the ladder in his hands, climbing upward. She followed him quickly, unwilling to lose the beautiful sight of his ass moving upward along the ladder. She wondered if that ass – most men didn't have one, and the ones who did, you couldn't stop looking at – she wondered if he got it from riding motorcycles or from good genetics or something else entirely.

Darrin was standing, stooping just a little beneath the low ceiling of the loft, by the time she got up.

'You should take off your shirt, if you don't want it to get dirty. And those pants, for sure.'

'Because you care about the cleanliness of my clothes?'

'In truth,' she said as she began to unbutton his prim and proper buttons. 'No. Because if this is your last clean outfit, and you get it dirty, then I get to see you walking around naked until you find the super-secret ...' She undid the last button and pushed the shirt back to expose his chest, letting her fingers spread out over his chin. 'Washer and dryer ...'

'The washer is super-secret?'

'Oh, yes,' she said. 'And so ...' She took his shirt all the way off, shook it and hung it on one of the tool hooks along the wall. '... you see why you must take everything off lest you get it very very dirty.'

'Your logic is escaping me,' he said, but he didn't stop her when she slid to her knees in the hay and reached to unbutton his jeans. He was already hard beneath his boxers, and she made quick work of them as well, delighting in the way his cock popped up as soon as it was free of its coverings. She took its length into her mouth, stretching her lips around him. He shifted his hips forward, urgent and rough, and she tasted the salt-sweet of him in the back of her throat.

'Kallie,' he said. 'Fuck.' His voice was rough-hewn and broken, more groans than words, and the very sound of it made her ache. Fuck, she wanted him. How did he keep doing this to her? Just when she thought she had this ... whatever it was ... in control, if nothing else, he turned the tables on her, ignited her desire with little more than a couple of words.

'Stop,' he said, tugging lightly at her hair. 'Wait ...'

The sensation of his hands, tight fingers wrapped in her hair, pulling her away, it left her breathless, wanting more. She sucked him in deeper, slipping her hand into her unbuttoned jeans, feeling the desire that soaked her fingers.

'Kallie,' he said again. 'Enough. God.'

This time, the tug was harder, insistent, and Kallie let herself be pulled away. She looked up at him, licking her lips, loving the dark heat that rimmed his blue eyes, the way his lids were hooded with lust as he looked down at her.

'You insouciant wench,' he said, and a grin almost broke through the words. 'It's my turn.'

Faster than she might have imagined, he was down in the hay with her, flipping her on her back. His fingers found her unbuttoned jeans, pushed her own hand away, then tugged down her jeans and underwear all in a single pull, until they were pooled around her ankles. His movements were rough with want, and that too, only deepened her desire. The hay that scratched her back and ass didn't do a thing to cool her want.

Especially not when he was leaning over her the way he was now, staring her down, lowering himself until he could set his mouth between her thighs, his tongue beginning long, slow strokes that bordered on torture. At the same time, his fingers found her and began to open her, resting inside so her that she ached and bucked upward into his touch, hoping that he would fill her with more, fill her more deeply, the sense of his weight inside her the only thing that offset the exquisite press of his tongue along her clit.

She loved oral sex, but normally, this was about the time she started feeling bad, wishing she could come but being unable to. She could feel herself reaching that point and tried to push past it, tried to imagine that he wasn't expecting anything from her, tried to tell herself that he was enjoying this as much as she'd enjoyed sucking him. Today, last night. Maybe tomorrow if he didn't get on his bike and ride.

He looked up at her from between her legs, his grin wicked, his lips wet with her. 'I could do this all day,' he said. 'You're beautiful.'

She felt that thing in her chest, cool as water, as liquid and immutable as a river. It didn't take away all of her worry, and it didn't mean that she could come, but it opened through her and let her breathe.

Darrin dipped his head again, resumed the twirls of his tongue, and then he pulled the length of her clit into his mouth. The tug was sharp and strong, and it surprised her enough that she let out a near-shout of pleasure.

He was making a sound of his own and she realised he was giggling. Between her legs. While he ate her out. That bastard. That–

And the he did the most surprising thing; he started circling the flesh of her ass with a finger, teasing her there, forcing her body to tense and squirm. She realised suddenly how long it had been since someone had touched her there, at all, and how much she'd missed it. He kept circling while his mouth worked the whole of her clit and just when she thought she couldn't stand it any more, she felt his finger enter her ass, soft and wet, a gentle push that filled her and stretched her and took her over the edge.

'Fuck, Darrin ...' She found his hair with her hands, fumbling and shaking, letting her orgasm rise up through her until it blurred her vision and stole her breath, until all she had left was pleasure and the feel of his body against hers.

Chapter Ten

DARRIN WAS FLOATING SOMEWHERE in-between asleep and awake, the delightful post-sex bliss that was made all that much better by Kallie's head on his chest, the scent of her – wood and leather and some sweet, unnameable fruit – in his nose. There was a piece of something – hay, straw, a stick? – poking him in the back, but he didn't care enough about it to actually move. If anything, the small discomfort made his pleasure all the better.

He could hear the puppy giving little puppy snores down below, and the sound of animals eating and moving about. But other than that, it was quiet. And still. He couldn't remember the last time he'd heard so little, felt so still. Peaceful. That was the word he was looking for. It felt ... he felt ... good. At home. Turning, he nuzzled against Kallie's neck, letting his mouth trace the soft curve of skin where it met her collarbone.

'Doorbell,' Kallie said, her voice sounding half-asleep.

And then, a second later, wide awake. 'Crap. Get dressed.'

'What?' he said. She scrambled up and was throwing clothes at him. He was pretty sure the shirt on his face was hers, although he couldn't remember her bringing it up with them.

'The horses only neigh when someone's here. Or if there's a coyote. Which there's not.' She pulled her shirt off his face and pulled it on. Even though he knew he was supposed to hurry – although he wasn't entirely sure for what – he was sad to see her body disappear beneath the fabric.

'This interruption is getting to be a bad habit,' he said. He sounded grumbly, but he knew it was only because of the waking up, because of how comfortable he'd been there in her arms. Nothing to worry about, nothing to decide.

'Come. On.' She tugged at his arm between words and he finally pulled himself up. Bits of stuff stuck to his back, and he swiped at them, but Kallie was already dressed and bopping down the ladder.

He climbed out of the hay loft far slower than she had, bits of hay still poking him in the ass under his jeans. He'd had to do something about that. Later.

Gauntlet was waiting at the bottom of the ladder, head cocked, clearly sure that something was up. He scooped him up in his arms and headed toward the barn door, expecting the man – did he even know his name? He realised he didn't – the man with his big truck.

Instead, it was Shar who met him at the barn door.

She grinned at him, lifting one reddish brow. 'Ah, there's the patient now. Kallie says she's been naughty-nursing you back to health.'

'I said no such thing!' From behind Shar, Kallie stood, arms folded across her chest. Her hair was full of straw and there was still rabbit fuzz all over her. God, she was cute when she was being a brat. He could sit here and watch the two of them all day. And he bet Shar could tell some amazing stories about her best friend. In fact, he bet she'd be all over that.

Shar rolled her eyes, canting her head at him. 'It's a good thing I can't hear her, isn't it? Come and let me look at your bite while you tell me all the dirty news about my favourite rescue friend.'

'I'm your only rescue friend!'

Shar lifted her brow in question and Darrin nodded in answer. 'Yes, she's bitching,' he said, although he was pretty sure Shar could hear every word that Kallie was saying.

He sat down on the hay bale farthest from Toddy's stall and pulled up his pant leg, having a bit of deja vu as he heard the horse stamping its feet behind him. Shar kneeled down and used her fingers to explore the bite. Only once did it hurt hard enough for him to clench his teeth together.

'Not bad,' she said. She turned to her friend, fingers flying, and a second later Kallie went off, all but stomping her feet and pouting.

'Giving her more shit about me?' he asked.

She watched his face intently, and it took him a second to remember she'd probably been reading his lips. She shook her head. 'No, I sent her on a silly errand so I could ask you what your intentions are with her.'

'I ... uh. What?'

She waited, as though she was expecting him to say more. He wasn't sure he had any more. He tried to dig into his thoughts on it, but it was a jumble of confusion between what she'd told him she'd needed – which was, clearly, not him – and what he could give and what he needed and ... He shook his head, willing his thoughts to settle before they exploded into a mulch of complete confusion.

'Let me try that again,' he said.

'I hoped you would.'

'Boy, I see why you two get along.'

Shar rewarded him with a smile, but didn't let him off the hook by saying anything.

'I'm here until I get the go-ahead from you to leave,' he said. 'She has the farm to take care of and I have, well ... I have a job to go back to.'

'That's what you want?'

Shar was doing something to the back of his leg that was both soothing and tingling, her fingers following the path of his aching and knotted calf.

'Does it matter ... Ow, God. What are you doing, amputating?'

'Not yet,' she said. 'But I could. I've never done one, but I hear they're not too bad ...'

'Funny,' he said.

'Do you think it's what she wants?' Shar asked, pushing herself up and pulling down his pant leg in a single, fluid motion. 'To be with a man she doesn't love?'

'I never asked her ... Wait. What?' For a second, he thought she meant him, but that was all wrong, right? They'd just met. Granted, they'd had great sex, great fantastic, oh my God hot sex, but love was a little fast, right? Except that he knew it wasn't. Not for him. The things he felt for her were beyond what he'd felt for someone in a long time.

Which is when the second part of Shar's question whacked him hard in the chest. To be with a man she didn't love? Clearly Shar didn't mean him.

'Oh,' he said as realisation hit him. 'She's going back to big-truck man ...' That's why she wanted him gone. That's why she'd said she had a solution. Was that also why she was fucking him, one last fling before she went back to the safety of a man who could save her farm? 'Crap,' he said.

'What?' Shar asked.

'I just realised what Kallie meant when she said–'

'When I said what?' Kallie was standing in the doorway, a tall man standing behind her. Darrin recognised him from the truck incident.

'Nothing,' Darrin said at the same time that Shar said something with her fingers that made both Kallie and the truck man scowl.

'Erik, this is Darrin. Darrin, Erik.'

'We've met,' Erik said, with a short nod in Darrin's direction. Darrin nodded back, finding his breath as stuck as his voice. He felt a stupid urge to challenge the man to a fist fight or an old-fashioned duel or something. Ridiculous. He'd known Kallie was going back to him. She'd told him. And he'd said yes anyway. The splitting of his heart that was happening in his chest, that was all his own fault.

'Somewhere we can talk, Kallie?' Erik said.

Neither Darrin nor Shar said anything more as they watched Kallie nod and lead Erik toward the house.

Chapter Eleven

DAMN BOYS. DAMN DOGS. Damn Shar.

It was a continual mantra, one that went around and around in Kallie's brain as she walked along the fence line, checking for down spots. Darrin was leaving. Hunting season was coming. Fall and Erik. Monetary safety and sadness of the heart, all tangled together.

She'd said no to Erik, that was the thing. Turned him down outright. Even if she couldn't have Darrin – and that was something she wasn't willing to think about, not yet, because she could feel the small tear happening in her heart, in her chest bones, in the place where she breathed and walked and lived and she knew it would kill her if she paid any attention to it at all – he'd shown her that she didn't have to settle. That somewhere there was a man who turned on her heart and her mind and her lust, who met her in all the ways she needed and wanted to be met.

So she'd done the impossible thing. She'd turned Erik down, and then she'd gone out to the barn to realise that Shar and Darrin had left. Darrin's motorcycle and camera were gone. They'd even taken Gauntlet. She didn't know what that meant, but she couldn't think about that right now either.

Finding a small hole, the wires bent by the heads of horses as they'd searched for good grass outside the fence, Kallie knelt to fix it, her hands working deftly at their task as her mind did the same with its own.

She'd figure out a way to save Safe Haven. Even if she had to sell off one of the back pastures, or a couple of acres of the woods. *I hope you can forgive me for that, Nana,* and she thought her nana would understand. 'Your land and your love are the two things you must always take care of,' Nana had always said. It seemed to Kallie that sometimes you had to choose one over the other. She could only hope she was choosing the right one.

She made her way along the pasture, stopping at places that didn't really need her attention, but unwilling to go back to the empty barn, the empty house. Unwilling to see the places where Darrin had stood or slept or held her. Unable to smell his scent in her house, see whatever objects he'd invariably left behind.

A soft rustle made her turn, still on her knees. Gauntlet, coming through the grass at a wriggly puppy pace, followed closely by Darrin. He held something behind his back, his grin so wide it nearly took up his whole face.

'Kallie,' he said. And there was something new in his voice.

'I quit my job.'

She didn't know how to respond to that. Tried to push herself up from her crouch and found herself floundering. The puppy seemed to think it was all a game, and tried clambering onto her lap.

'What?' she said. Which was only a quarter of all that was happening in her brain.

'Yeah,' he said. He came to her and pulled her up with one hand, Gauntlet curling into the crook of her curved arm as she rose. 'I quit. I feel amazing. I should have done that so long ago. But I just didn't, well, you helped me see that I didn't have to go back to it. That I could do what I loved and still–'

'That's great,' she said, interrupting, trying to get him to stop talking. She knew she should have been excited for him – he was holding her by the arms, he was right in front of her, and still she could barely swallow around the heavy thrum of her heart. 'I'm really glad for you.' And she was, but he was still leaving and she was still broke and feeling broken and all she wanted was to crush herself against him and beg him not to go. Still, she stood straight, held herself up, even though she felt like the world was spinning.

'I want to show you something,' he said.

He brought his camera out from behind his back, and turned it toward her. It took a second for her to realise what she was seeing: An image of her and Toddy, the big horse taking a carrot from her hand, his velvet-soft lips carefully moving over her palm, his eyes half-closed, her own grin wider than she'd realised.

'I didn't know you were there for that,' she said.

'And more,' he said. 'Here.'

He handed her the camera and she flipped through the images. Her and Gauntlet playing in the grass. The horses running wild across the green. The sun coming slant over the barn in the morning. One of angoras, caught in motion, sniffing at Gauntlet through the wire cage. With each one her heart broke, but also levied. It was as though he'd captured everything she loved about the farm. As though he'd somehow captured her very heart in pictures.

'They're beautiful,' she said.

'I forgot what I loved,' he said. 'You reminded me.'

Kallie flipped to a new picture, one of her, lying in bed naked, the puppy curled against her. She looked at peace. She looked like she was home.

Tears came, unbidden, warm against the chill of her face.

'Well, you're not really supposed to cry about that.'

'I know,' she said, trying not to sniffle.

'So,' he said. 'What do you think?'

Think? About what? 'They're beautiful.'

'No,' he said. 'About using them. For the farm. To save the farm.'

'What?'

'I don't want you to sell or rent or give anything to the big truck man,' he said. 'I want you. I want to be here with

209

you. I want to help you with the farm – even with that damn horse that bit me, because, yeah, that hurt, but if that hadn't happened, I wouldn't still be here.'

Kallie shook her head, confused. What was he talking about?

'I already said no to Erik.'

'Oh,' he said. 'That's even better. Say yes to me then.'

'I don't understand.'

'The pictures. We can sell them, turn them into postcards, photos, T-shirts, hell, I don't care. There's so much beauty here. People want more beauty in their lives. They need it. They forget every day. We'll remind them.'

Kallie stood, stone-faced. Her breath was stuck somewhere between her heart and her mouth. She could feel her heart beating in her wrists. The things he was saying, were they even an option? To have the farm, and him, and whatever this thing was with photos?

'Shar gave me the idea,' he said. 'So if it sucks, you can blame her.'

'She did?'

'Yes,' he said. 'The photo idea anyway. The other idea, I came up with all on my own.'

'What other idea?'

'To love you, of course,' he said.

'You love me?' Was she ever going to say something smart? Where was her brain, her breath?

'Duh,' he said, which made her laugh and then breathe and then she could speak and move forward to wrap her arms around him. He hugged her back, the camera swinging behind her and hitting her in the ass.

'Can we really do that? Support the farm with photos?'

'Are you questioning my talent?' he asked. 'Besides, Shar said if that didn't work we could do a nude charity calendar. You know, shave the rabbits and stuff.'

'I'm going to have to thank her for that one too,' Kallie said.

'OK, fine, that may have been my idea.'

'Jerk,' she said.

'Yes,' he said. 'Now, do you suppose we can have wild, fantastic sex without one interruption or another? Because that would be really, really nice.'

'Let's see what we can do about that,' she said. 'But not out here.'

He pouted, in that sweet way she loved, and she leaned in and kissed his lower lip, a soft nibble that brought back all the desire she'd been carrying for him, let it sweep over her and into him. Would this thing work? She didn't know. But she felt, for the first time in a long time, that she was not just exactly where she needed to be, but that her heart was too.

She knelt and scooped Gauntlet up in one arm.

'Race you home,' she said.

'You're already home,' he said, laughing. But he ran after her anyway, ran after her and caught her and kissed her in the strong, warm circle of his arms.

'So are you,' she said.

Epilogue

'YOU'RE DOING GREAT, BIG boy,' Kallie told the newest recruit, a young Thoroughbred who'd arrived just last week. She'd stalled the colt with Toddy, and right now the big horse was doing his best to calm the baby. How far he'd come. How far they'd all come.

Kallie held out a carrot to Toddy, and he came to her and lipped it off her palm as she brushed his mane out of his eyes. He no longer bit, and in truth, he was ready to go to a new home, but she had decided to keep him here, at Safe Haven. If it hadn't been for him, she wouldn't have Darrin and Gauntlet. She wouldn't have Safe Haven. She wouldn't even have herself.

Slipping out of the stall, she shut the door and smiled at the payment schedule written on the barn blackboard. The bank had given them more time to pay, and in the end, they hadn't needed it. Darrin's photos had sold not just to people who wanted beauty in their lives, but to a couple of big companies Darrin knew from his LA work, who'd wanted them for ads. The farm was hers, would always be hers. And Darrin had said he'd stay as long as she'd have him. Which in her mind was a very long time.

As she crossed the lawn toward the house, she saw Darrin sitting on the front porch. He had a camera in his lap, but he was just looking out at the horses in the pasture. Gauntlet was asleep on the step between his legs, already growing out of his puppyhood, his muzzle resting on Darrin's shoe. The two of them looked like they belonged there, more than anything had ever belonged at Safe Haven.

Kallie was overwhelmed by a sudden urge to drop everything and run to them both. Instead, she forced herself to stroll slowly, to experience the pleasure of watching them come closer and closer as she neared.

'Your smile gives you away,' Darrin said, his own smile making an appearance.

'I don't know what you're talking about,' she said.

But of course, she did. She knew exactly what he meant. And he knew it – he crooked his pointer finger at her as if taking an invisible picture, the cursive tattoo now clearly readable along his curved skin. *Smile.*

Kallie sat down on the steps beside him, her leg touching his, one hand reaching down to ruffle the pup's ears. Darrin reached across her and kissed her, and she leaned into his mouth with a quiet sigh of contentment and want. Between their feet, Gauntlet yawned without opening his eyes, then rose and turned three circles on the step before plopping back down, his tail thumping the wood.

Home, the wagging tail seemed to say. *Home.*

More great titles in
The Secret Library

Traded Innocence
9781908262028

Silk Stockings
9781908262042

The Thousand and One Nights
9781908262080

The Game
9781908262103

Hungarian Rhapsody
9781908262127

The Thousand and One Nights – Kitti Bernetti

When Breeze Monaghan gets caught red-handed by her millionaire boss she knows she's in trouble. Big time. Because Breeze needs to keep her job more than anything else in the world. Sebastian Dark is used to getting exactly what he wants and now he has a hold over Breeze, he makes her an offer she can't refuse. Like Scheherazade in The 1001 Nights Seb demands that Breeze entertain him to save her skin. Can she employ all her ingenuity and sensuality in order to satisfy him and stop her world crashing about her? Or, like the ruthless businessman he is, will Seb go back on the deal?

Out of Focus – Primula Bond

Eloise Stokes's first professional photography assignment seems to be a straightforward family portrait. But the rich, colourful Epsom family – father Cedric, step-mother Mimi, twin sons Rick and Jake, and sister Honey – are intrigued by her understated talent and she is soon sucked into their wild world. As the initial portrait sitting becomes an extended photo diary of the family over an intense, hot weekend, Eloise gradually blossoms until she is equally happy in front of the lens.

The Highest Bidder – Sommer Marsden

Recent widow Casey Briggs is all about her upcoming charity bachelor auction. She doesn't have time for dating. Her heart isn't strong enough yet. But when one of their bachelors is arrested and she finds herself a hunky guy short, she employs her best friend Annie to find her a new guy pronto.

Enter Nick Murphy – handsome, kind, and not very hard to look at, thank you very much. And he quickly makes her feel things she hasn't felt in a while. A very long while. Casey's not sure if she's ready for it – the whole moving on thing. But as she prepares to auction Nick off, she's discovering that her first hunch was correct – he's damn near priceless.

The Game – Jeff Cott

The Game is the story of Ellie's bid to change from sexy, biddable housewife to sexy dominant goddess.

Ellie and Jake are a happily married couple who play a bedroom game. Having lost the last Game Ellie must start the new one where she left off – bound and gagged on the bed. As she figures out how to tie herself up before Jake's return from work, Ellie remembers the last Game and has ideas for the new one. Jake is immensely strong and loving and has seemingly endless sexual stamina so the chances of Ellie truly gaining control look slim. Although she has won the Game on occasions, she suspects he lets her win just so he can overwhelm her in the next. She has to find a way to break this pattern.

But does she succeed?

One of Us – Antonia Adams

Successful artist Natalie Crane is midway through a summer exhibition with friend and agent Anton when Will Falcon strolls tantalisingly into her life. After a messy divorce, a relationship is not Natalie's priority. Anton takes an immediate dislike to the shaven-headed composer, but Natalie is captivated. He is everything she is not: free, impulsive and seemingly with no thought for the future. He introduces her to Dorset's beautiful coves and stunning countryside and their time together is magical.

Things get complicated when her most famous painting, a nude self-portrait, is stolen and there are no signs of a break-in. When it's time for her return to London, Will doesn't turn up to say goodbye, and she cannot trace him. Anton tells her to forget him, but she cannot. Then she discovers the stakes are much higher than they first appeared.

Taste It – Sommer Marsden

Jill and Cole are competing for the title of *Best Chef*. The spicy, sizzling and heated televised contest fuels a lust in Jill she'd rather keep buried. She can't be staring at the man's muscles ... he's her competition! During a quick cooking throwdown things start to simmer and it becomes harder and harder for Jill to ignore that she's smitten in the kitchen. Cole's suggestive glances and sly smiles aren't helping her any. When fate puts her in his shower and then his chivalrous nature puts her in his borrowed clothes, there's no way to deny the natural heat between them.

Hungarian Rhapsody – Justine Elyot

Ruby had no idea what to expect from her trip to Budapest, but a strange man in her bed on her first night probably wasn't it. Once the mistake is ironed out, though, and introductions made, she finds herself strangely drawn to the handsome Hungarian, despite her vow of holiday celibacy. Does Janos have what it takes to break her resolve and discover the secrets she is hiding, or will she be able to resist his increasingly wild seduction tactics? Against the romantic backdrop of a city made for lovers, personalities clash. They also bump. And grind.

Restraint – Charlotte Stein

Marnie Lewis is certain that one of her friends – handsome but awkward Brandon – hates her guts. The last thing she wants to do is go on a luscious weekend away with him and a few other buddies, to a cabin in the woods. But when she catches Brandon doing something very dirty after a night spent listening to her relate some of her *sexcapades* to everyone, she can't resist pushing his buttons a little harder. He might seem like a prude, but Marnie suspects he likes a little dirty talk. And Marnie has no problems inciting his long dormant desires.

A Sticky Situation – Kay Jaybee

If there is a paving stone to trip over, or a drink to knock over, then Sally Briers will trip over it or spill it. Yet somehow Sally is the successful face of marketing for a major pharmaceutical company; much to the disbelief of her new boss, Cameron James.

Forced to work together on a week-long conference in an Oxford hotel, Sally is dreading spending so much time with arrogant new boy Cameron, whose presence somehow makes her even clumsier than usual.

Cameron, on the other hand, just hopes he'll be able to stay professional, and keep his irrational desire to lick up all the accidentally split food and drink that is permanently to be found down Sally's temptingly curvy body, all to himself.

Silk Stockings – Constance Munday

When Michael Levenstein meets Imogen, an exotic dancer at a Berlin nightclub, a passionate and intense love story develops. Michael becomes obsessed by mysterious Imogen and falls into a world of intense sexual fantasy and desire. But Imogen is determined to protect a personal, dark secret at all costs and because of this she has forbidden herself love.

With Imogen afraid of committing and afraid of losing what she has fought for so desperately, can Michael break down her barriers and discover a solution to his lover's deep dark secret, thus freeing the enigmatic Imogen to truly love him?

The Lord of Summer – Jenna Bright

Banished to the back of beyond, in the middle of a long, hot summer, Gem and Dan Parker find their marriage filling up with secrets. As they work to reopen the Green Man pub, tensions and unacknowledged desires come between them. From their first night, when Gem sees someone watching them make love from the edge of the woods, her fantasies of having two men at once start to grow and consume her. As the temperature rises, she becomes fixated by her imaginings of an impossible, gorgeous, otherworldly man in the forest. A man who could make her dreams come true – and maybe save her marriage.

Off the Shelf – Lucy Felthouse

At 35, travel writer Annalise is fed up with insensitive comments about being left "on the shelf". It's not as if she doesn't *want* a man, but her busy career doesn't leave her much time for relationships. Sexy liaisons with passing acquaintances give Annalise physical satisfaction but she needs more than that. She wants a man who will satisfy her mind as well as her body. But where will she find someone like that?

It seems Annalise may be in luck when a new member of staff starts working in the bookshop at the airport she regularly travels through. Damien appears to tick all the boxes – he's gorgeous, funny and intelligent, and he shares Annalise's love of books and travel.

The trouble is, Damien's shy and Annalise is terrified of rejection. Can they overcome their fears and admit their feelings, or are they doomed to remain on the shelf?